# A
# FAIRY TALE

# A FAIRY TALE

PAULINE GAVIN

ILLUSTRATION BY KELLY BARROW

authorHOUSE®

AuthorHouse™ UK Ltd.
1663 Liberty Drive
Bloomington, IN 47403   USA
www.authorhouse.co.uk
Phone: 0800.197.4150

Published by AuthorHouse    05/07/2013

ISBN: 978-1-4817-9045-1 (sc)
ISBN: 978-1-4817-9046-8 (e)

To the greatest fairy of them all,
Anna

# Acknowledgements

I would like to acknowledge my schoolmaster, Mr. Cornelius Egan, who instilled in me a love of writing, and my English teacher, Mrs. Mary Staunton, who nurtured that love.

I would also like to thank my parents for their encouragement and Fraser for listening.

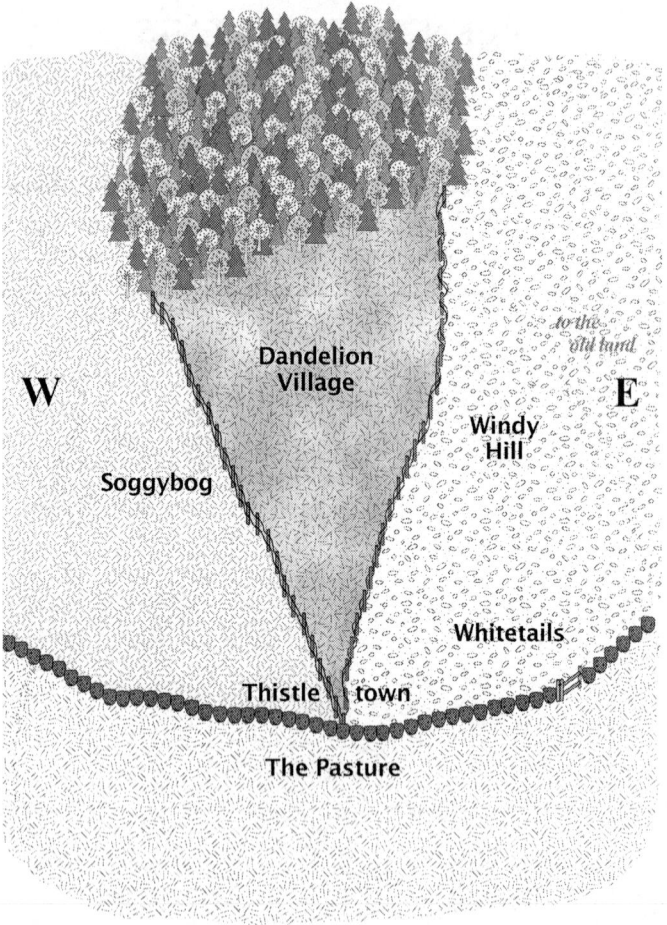

N
to the mountains

W

E

to the old land

Dandelion
Village

Windy
Hill

Soggybog

Whitetails

Thistle    town

The Pasture

S

# THE FENCE AND THE HEDGEROW

Daylight slipped through musty autumn rain, highlighting in pale orange, a hill, a forest, and a wide waste, tall with bull rushes. The wet soil was brown with fallen leaves and rich in nutrition, perfect for fairies that had walked a tired, heartbroken way, carrying wings that were flightless since anyone could remember. While the others slept, one fairy stood alone, surveying the landscape. In the north stood the dark forest, and south lay the good land, the pasture. In the west, where they had never been, he saw flat land; in the east, the high hill over which they came and, beyond that, the land he convinced them to leave. The fairy, Uulor, turned around and gazed upon his sleeping charges. In the fairy lore, one alone guarded them from hurt, leading the way forward, and Uulor remembered with a pang of regret how fun his life had been before the council named him for the task. Uulor never chose that role for himself, but here he was, in the same moment feared and revered—lonely when alone, lonely when surrounded by the multitude.

The earth became bright; the rain stopped, and Uulor spoke. 'Golden Orb[1] has risen. Feather-bills[2] are singing.'

The fairies awoke to the light of Golden Orb, cursing her early dawn as they had cursed her setting hours before, when

---

[1]    Golden Orb is the sun.

[2]    Feather-bills are birds, usually small ones.

darkness impeded their way. They shook themselves and listened as a populace to his words.

'A quiet place is what we need,' he explained, 'away from men and their works.'

Many thistles were spread across the wide space. The lea was a white, billowy mass such as the fairies had never seen before, and thistle seeds were constantly floating by, tickling the wind. Only in a magical world could such a place exist, they thought. The whole scene was beautifully calm, and the fairies were taken in as though a spell had been put upon them. They lay again to rest, and journeyed no more. Uulor stood watch as they lay.

He talked to the thistles, and the ragwort, and the blades of grass, and while the fairies rested, the weeds began to whisper back to him. Thistles and dandelions enjoyed the most respect in the hierarchy of weeds. They were the 'high weeds,' and they held most sway in all that occurred.

Over time, the fairies brought a new kind of life, for they could understand the words of weeds though they spoke a foreign tongue, and every blade of grass they swung from, every leaf on which they stood, felt a thrill at their touch and shone with renewed lustre, for theirs was the mythical blood, though they had no knowledge of the magic of their bones or the force of their touch. But the curious weeds learnt little of the world beyond from the fairies, who were so weary that it was a long time before they could explore. At first, the fairies knew nothing of the grassy, mossy Inner Lea with its delicate flowers. Instead, they huddled together and were cramped, where the fence and the hedgerow meet.

There occurred to the thistles a bright idea, which would later come to benefit fairies to no end. They thought, 'If the fairies are so tired, why don't they ride on the backs of our seeds and let the wind take them to the ends of the lea? They can find a nice place to live, and they need weary themselves no more.'

The fairies agreed that this was a wonderful idea, so they chose from among them one who would brave the venture first. This chosen fairy was called Barzad, and he had a wild nature, loving his friends with a passion. Not blessed with a pleasant personality, he was grumpy, stern, arrogant, dark, and brooding. Concentration was his specialty. He thought with his hands, looking through the steeple of his fingers. Many times during his journey, Barzad had been made to curtail his feistiness, so he was keen to prove his worth now in front of the multitude. He climbed to the highest peak of the prickliest thistle he could find and waited for the wind to take him. A seed quivered beneath him, and in a few moments he was blown away into the breeze.

Down below on the surface of the soil, the fairies shuddered, fearing for his safety. They knew nothing of the breeze and its ways and worried that they might never see Barzad again. But Barzad was not far away. From up in the air he looked down at all his friends. Then he turned around and could see the whole lea. He saw Golden Orb high above and many seeds beside him. He saw the huge congregation of thistles and the barriers[3], strong and unfamiliar. Another gust of wind and he was among the daisies and speedwell of Inner Lea, where he had never been. He was gently lowered onto the ground, where he sat on a dog daisy. He rested a while and soon was borne again into the air towards the marsh where the rushes waded, their long, skinny legs bare against the water. From there, he was blown towards Gloomy Forest where the oak trees stood. The light of Golden Orb could not penetrate the heavy branches, so the forest floor looked dark and uninviting. This made Barzad afraid, and he was glad to be blown away back to the thistles and his friends.

He landed softly on a tuft of moss and came down from the seed. He told all his friends of what he had seen. Some liked the sound of Inner Lea where the scented flowers grew and chose

---

[3]    Barriers are usually manmade (fences, walls, gates, etc.).

to live there. Dandelions also lived there, and the fairies were their friends, so they were called the dandelion fairies. Some wanted to live in the marsh with its gangly reeds. These became the marsh fairies, and they grew to love Soggybog[4] and the buttercup patches where they made their homes. Some wanted to stay by their thistle hosts, so they made home with thistles and were cramped no more. These were the thistle fairies.

Some fairies chose none of these places but decided to wander alone. They were the lone fairies. They wanted a simple life with no rules and no leaders. Bur-duun was one of these, but soon after the fairies segregated, she left the lone life to live with thistles. Bor'Tem was her sister, and she lived in Thistle Town also. Scuri'Boo was lone, but he was a sociable fairy and could be found anywhere in the lea. He knew how to read the leaves in the way that we read tarot cards. He spoke to the whitetails[5] and dreamt of many ways to outwit men. During their segregation, Uulor remained quiet, believing his tiresome work to be done. Many turned to him for guidance, unsure of where they should make home and what their future was, but he let them make their own decisions. He hid from them, deep in the dark places. Some fairies made wrong decisions and changed their minds, but they learned from their mistakes in a way that Uulor could never have taught them. The respect that he had earned was short-lived, and some strong fairies, such as Barzad, were glad he kept himself alone because his dark tales of men scared them. Still, they followed him, because he was never yet wrong, tired and grey as he was. Soon all fairies had found comfortable homes, and they were glad to rest, having travelled so far, unnoticed and undiminished in number, a miracle, really. So that is how it came to pass that the fairies were dispersed throughout the lea and for a while, all fairies lived in peace and were tranquil.

---

[4]    Soggybog is the fairy name for the bog land beyond the fence.

[5]    Whitetails are rabbits.

Thistle fairies quickly settled by the fringes on Windy Hill. They had no need to go in search of a home, for they chose to stay where they were. They were many, and they rode the seed for fun and adventure. They believed that the riding of seeds was a magical gift given to them by the high weeds, so they chose for leader Barzad, bravest of fairies, who was first to ride. They believed themselves to be the most wonderful of all fairies, and often they would ride in unison, creating a huge, white cloud of thistle seeds so that none could fail to notice their greatness. Barzad was youthful and vibrant, and he loved the thistle fairies, for they were brave and wild like he. Over time Thistle Town grew, and many fairies came to join, so the season of thistles was a lively affair. The fairies would celebrate their thistledom, and many from outside Thistle Town would come and watch the festival.

If thistle fairies were fond of a cultural affair, dandelions were even more so. There is not a fairy folk song that didn't originate from a dandelion, and their poetry is popular among all. Dandelion fairies chose Tu'Hob to be their leader, for he was the Kazma-zan, or chief speaker of the fairy council, who were keepers of the fairy lore. The fairy council began long ago, when they still lived in the far place beyond the lea, but as the unknown began to descend that Uulor could not ignore, they felt powerless and sought to protect themselves, and the influence of the council waned. So, unsupported and unnoticed the council continued documenting their histories, working tirelessly to keep them remembered.

Tu'Hob was pale and small, and looked older than his years. Curly wisps of golden hair almost covered his little eyes, which were close together on his skinny face. He was a reader and a philosopher, and his education earned him respect from his elders. De'Lyza was a council elder, and the long journey made him weary, but dandelion life was convalescent, so he chose to stay there. When the fairies first settled in Inner Lea, the dandelions were seedless. It was the season of thistles, and it would be a long time before the fairies knew that dandelions were like thistles, in that their seeds could be ridden in the wind.

Soggybog was damp and cold, and save for the beauty of buttercups all would have been unwelcoming. Marsh fairies preferred not to ride the seed but to travel as they always had, prancing lightly from reeds to rushes and swinging by the blades of grass. They chose for their leader Wui-bur, who was most reluctant to ride the seed. He believed the seeds belonged only to the high weeds, who shared their seeds just until the fairies found a place that was not cramped, that continuing to ride them might bring misfortune, and that the high weeds could put a spell on unsuspecting fairies, though it was actually they, who possessed the greater gifts.

The fairies could not sense their part in the miracles taking place around them, so when a flower burst into bloom at the touch of a fairy or when a fallen leaf retained its orange beauty unlike its friends who decayed into the ground, the fairies believed this to be the work of high weeds and carried on their way as little fireworks of colour exploded behind them. Wui-bur's grandfather was Vi'Shay, eldest of all fairies, and they resembled each other in mind. Both were likable, carefree, young at heart, and a little immature, though Wui-bur could be forgiven in his youth.

Buttercups were dotted all over Soggybog, and the fairies lived with them and slept on their waxy, yellow petals. They worshipped the buttercups, believing their petals were brighter even than Golden Orb herself and that sleeping on them would bring youth; after all, Wui-bur himself was only a child in the eyes of most fairies. Many frogs lived in Soggybog, and the fairies came to love their constant croaking and jumping about. It was the jumping and hopping of frogs that inspired the marsh fairies to dance, and the season of frogspawn was filled with dances performed in honour of 'hopping greens', their hosts; for the fairies knew that they were not first to settle in the marsh, nor indeed anywhere in the lea, and they were ever grateful to the weeds and creatures that welcomed them. They were careful of webs and the spiders that spun them, but web-weavers[6] seldom posed a threat. They were also wary of feather-bills, who might inadvertently peck and injure them as they dug for worms, but marsh fairies had little fear of them, as the feather-bills of Soggybog ate only by the bendy river where silver-slithers[7] lived.

---

[6]   Web-weavers are spiders.

[7]   Silver-slithers are fish.

# Stooping Reed

Wui-bur loved Soggybog. Here he could swing and prance between the reeds and grasses as they all used to do in times past. And the buttercups! Even on a dull day the buttercups would bloom, making everyone feel bright and beautiful. How lovely it was to see their petals bend under the weight of a fairy: over the top would peer two little eyes that Wui-bur would recognise.

Yes, Wui-bur loved Soggybog. But there were times when he would rather be alone, so one morning when Golden Orb was not yet bright, Wui-bur went wandering. Most of the fairies were still fast asleep, but Vi'Shay was up already, preening and splashing in the shallow waters. They had spoken recently of a thistle who desired to come and stay for a while with the marshes, so Vi'Shay stopped washing while his grandchild leader came to him.

'This thistle friend of yours, Vi'Shay?'

'Yes. Bor'Tem is her name.'

'Ah! Bor'Tem. I know her.'

'She serves on the council.'

Wui-bur was surprised. 'A thistle on the council! Does Barzad know?'

'Barzad pays little heed to Bor'Tem, and what Barzad doesn't know she won't tell him. Anyway, our friend Bor'Tem is well able for him.'

Now Wui-bur was intrigued. Any fairy who could stand up to Barzad was a fairy worth meeting. 'Tell Bor'Tem we'd love her to come.'

Vi'Shay finished washing and, finding some tasty seeds, sat down for a little nibble. When Golden Orb had risen over Windy Hill, he set out on his way to Thistle Town. If he got there early enough, he could have Bor'Tem in the marsh before nightfall. Wui-bur set out also, and he was soon at the edge of the marsh where the tall grasses grow.

During his absence, the marshes were celebrating, for great joy was theirs. Dun'Nur and Dun'Mee awoke to find a new baby born to them. It was a fine, strong boy, large for a fairy, pulling and bending the reeds of their home. They called him Stooping Reed on account of his enormous size and the landscape he was born into. Dun'Mee pulled him close and stroked his little handsome head. Dun'Nur repaired the reed ceiling, which had just been torn asunder. He really must extend their home—upwards. They offered the child berries and bark, but it seemed he had already fed himself, so the three sat looking at each other with grins on their happy faces. Whispers were heard outside, and a crowd were gathering at a respectable distance. News spread fast in Soggybog, but some were still unaware. Vi'Shay could not be found, for he was gone to bring Bor'Tem from Thistle Town and 'Where is Wui-bur?' many asked. The young chief had not been seen all morning.

Wui-bur was by now outside Gloomy Forest, where he had slept and was beginning to stir. Not far away, beneath the leaves of a violet, there lay another fairy. Her name was Fari-bur. She was a lone fairy and knew nothing of Wui-bur and his marsh friends. Having woken, she climbed onto the violet petals, where the dew was still wet, and washed herself. That done, she scrambled down and made for the woods for breakfast. A few roots and freshly fallen bark would suffice, for berries were dangerous to eat where many feather-bills lived. Nearby, Wui-bur stretched and rubbed his eyes. Daylight had moved behind the trees, and all was shade. Web-weavers had been out, and their webs were everywhere. If he moved he might become entangled. Afraid, he closed his eyes and prayed to Golden Orb but his prayers were answered, instead, by a tiny voice.

'Are you lost?'

'Oh no, I always come here.' He was lying, trying to save face. 'I'm Wui-bur of the marshes.'

'And I'm Fari-bur. I live in the forest.'

'What? On your own? In Gloomy Forest?' Wui-bur was horrified.

'Well, I am a lone fairy, and the forest is a beautiful place,' she said. 'I love to climb the branches and snooze on the moss. See the mushrooms growing on the bark? Aren't they wonderful?'

She showed him all the wondrous things that could be found: how to look for Golden Orb between the branches, how the purple violets slumbered in the shade, how to find the furry creatures that scrambled in the bushes. She introduced him to Learned, the acorn, who lived with the mighty oak trees, and showed him how the river looked in the shady green banks. They stayed a while eating bark and nuts, and when she had showed him everything they pranced into the lea, leaving the forest behind. Ragwort was standing by the barrier, deep in conversation with a nettle. They kept going until they reached the marsh, but Fari-bur grew afraid.

'I've never been to the marsh.'

He ignored her whine and led her on, stopping only when he got to Ferny arch, which was his home. Fari-bur saw that he had many friends and that he was a leader of fairies, even at his young age. The crowd were still gathered around Dun'Nur and Dun'Mee, and Wui-bur was told the great news. He crept quietly over to where Stooping Reed lay sleeping on a buttercup leaf, dreaming of reeds and nectar. Vi'Shay had returned early, with Bor'Tem. She was unlike most thistles, relaxed and easy-going. She complimented the young chief on his choice of home, for Soggybog was indeed a wonderful place and had much to offer the fairies.

Many had turned their attention to the beautiful Fari-bur, who would not leave Wui-bur's side, and when politely asked who she was, she explained all about herself and Gloomy Forest. They were keen to see the lovely things that Fari-bur talked of, so she agreed to lead an expedition to the forest, but first she would spend a while with the fairies of Soggybog.

One evening, the fairy council met. There was Tu'Hob, Vi'Shay, Bor'Tem, Uulor, Boo, and Scuri'Boo. Many other fairies served on the council but couldn't make it. Dun'Nur was busy rebuilding his home, and De'Lyza was tired. Those who were there, proposed a new system where everyone could spend time in Dandelion Village and learn all the wonderful histories that made them who they are. But when this idea was put to the populace, not everyone agreed, and some openly opposed it. Barzad was one of these. He believed that reminding fairies of the long journey and the world before it would instil fear into the hearts of many who were weak already. Tu'Hob, as Kazma-zan, believed that fairies should not forget who they were or where they came from. The two leaders could not come to an agreement, and it made all the fairies unhappy. Barzad could not explain his reasons for disliking the idea, but he felt apprehension throughout the lea like a dark cloud hovering while a storm brewed within. Something was wrong; he could see it and touch it, but he knew not what it was or how to change it. The fairies did not recognise their own magic, so how could they see when it was weakened? Their power was diminished, so that sometimes the wild blossoms of nature remained unchanged when the fairies brushed by them, and there was greyness.

During this time there lived in Thistle Town a fairy unlike his friends, whose name was Ben'Tork. He was mild of nature and a little past youth, but his heart was young and he had great, enduring love for all fairies. He knew many poems; he and his blade-whistle were popular throughout the lea, but especially in Thistle Town, where his gentleness was refreshing against the dark thoughts of moody Barzad. Despite their many differences of character, Barzad and Ben'Tork were the closest of friends. When the fairies had first come to the lea, Ben'Tork wanted only to live with Barzad and enjoy the life of thistles, but now that many fairies had ventured out to further regions, he could see that the thistle way was neither the only way nor, indeed, the best. As time went on, Ben'Tork began to spend time with Tu'Hob in Dandelion Village, where the poetry of the past was a thing of the present and the fairies were gentle and calm. Dandelion was a sleepy little village in comparison to the busy towers Ben'Tork was used to, and the more time he spent away from Thistle Town, the greater was his reluctance to return.

Tu'Hob invited Ben'Tork to sit on the fairy council, which made him glad because he believed that dandelions were right not to forget the past. Barzad, however, was disappointed. He knew it was only a matter of time before Ben'Tork left Thistle Town for good. One morning Ben'Tork returned from a visit to Inner Lea. He was summoned to Thorny Tunnel, which was Barzad's home, and went immediately, seeing this as his best chance to explain to his friend and chief. To his surprise, Barzad made it easy for him. When he arrived, Barzad was sitting alone, with a nutshell of nectar and some tasty new buds to nibble on.

'Ben'Tork, my friend. You are sentimental, and I often wondered why you chose the way of thistles.' Ben'Tork was instantly relaxed.

'So do I, Barzad; and now Tu'Hob has invited me to sit on the council. I think it would suit me better because I cannot forget the past. You look to the future, brave Barzad, while the rest of us are afraid. Are you not afraid of anything?'

'My fear is that fairies won't progress and that we will keep wandering and straying as we have done. The council is useless to us now, when we must move forward. I believe that no fairy born in Weedy Lea should be told of the past and the world we have fled. I'd rather that they live for the future alone.'

'It seems sensible to me,' said Ben'Tork. 'In the marsh there is progress. The worship of buttercups takes their minds away from the past. Vi'Shay was weary from the journey, but now he is well again, and many say it is because the buttercups bring youth.'

'Yes,' Barzad said, making a steeple with his hands. 'You know, when I first saw Soggybog, I hated it, never wanted to go there.' But in his mind he was saying, 'Wui-bur is wise. Perhaps I should have given him more credit.'

Barzad and Ben'Tork sat together for most of the day. The conversation moved onto Bur-duun, Bor'Tem's sister, who had come to live in Thistle Town. Barzad described her in detail. Ben'Tork could tell from Barzad's tone that she had made a lasting impression on him. Barzad was quite happy to welcome her, for secretly he thought she was beautiful, and if she stayed, it would indeed be a consolation for the departure of Ben'Tork.

The talk moved back to the council's proposal, and a decision was made. All fairies born hereafter would be given new lea names unlike the names of the old tongue. Those who chose to learn more of their past could do so, but first they must earn the right by serving time on the council. This suited Barzad, who believed that few would willingly serve, so most would remain ignorant of the wrongs done them by men.

Ben'Tork left him, and he became thoughtful. He placed a leaf over the opening of Thorny Tunnel to show that no visitors would be accepted. He really must get an assistant to do all that, he thought—Kuz'Aar, perhaps. Now that the door was closed, darkness surrounded him. Good; it suited his mood. Ben'Tork would be gone soon, and Barzad could feel a large, gaping hole being slowly dug into him. Was this what loneliness felt like? If so, he must try to be kind to Bur-duun, for she had done something to him, and he could not remove her from his mind.

A chill filled the little dark chamber, and Barzad knew it was evening. He thought for a while about the shade that had come to surround him. Strangely, Uulor seemed not to notice the feeling. Indeed, it was only Barzad who noticed. He had never understood it, nor would he come close tonight, so he curled up beneath the thistles for sleep that would long elude him.

# A TRIP TO THE MARSH

Ever since he arrived at the lea, Barzad's fear of Gloomy Forest could not be assuaged. The thought of feather-bills and sinister noises brought him almost to the point of panic. He was alone in this fear, and to make it worse, Wui-bur had gone there and come back with Fari-bur, the lone, who lived there. How anyone could sleep in such a place he couldn't understand, but one thing was certain: he must learn to face Gloomy Forest. For Barzad the brave, leader of thistles, first to ride the seed, to be afraid of the shadows of Gloomy Forest was ridiculous. He must not give the fairies something to laugh at, especially not the marsh fairies. He had to learn more about Gloomy Forest and the lone fairy Fari-bur. He thought aloud, 'Bor'Tem went to the marsh. She likes to study the lea; she would surely have it all chronicled in her diary.' So he appointed Kuz'Aar his helper and sent him after her to request a full report. Bor'Tem would be thrilled because it meant she could research both the marsh and the forest and stay as long as she wanted. Not that she disliked her life as a thistle—he knew that. In fact, she had a great regard for Barzad. Kuz'Aar was not so happy at the prospect of making the journey all the way to drizzly, dull Soggybog, but go he did, for he too had respect for Barzad, though his was more of the fear variety. Kuz'Aar was also disappointed that he had to leave just as Bur-duun arrived. The two had connected as soon as they met, and he would rather stay and get to know her better. But all the fairies loved her, and she would surely settle in Thistle Town; he would have plenty of time to spend with Bur-duun later.

Earlier that morning, Uulor felt great joy in the water and instinctively went to Soggybog. He knew nothing of Stooping Reed coming into the world, bringing hope to all fairies. Had he known the good news, he would have savoured the relief that came with it, but he was afraid. What if he had led all the fairies to the wrong place? What if it was a dangerous place? The whitetails had recently spied men. What if Weedy Lea was a land of men? Scuri'Boo feared the same thing, and the whitetail chief, Big-buck, thought it best to dig new runs close to Thistle Town, where men seldom go, but Barzad objected on the grounds that it would endanger the fairies.

Scuri'Boo knew the whitetails were right, so he went to find Bor'Tem in Soggybog. She would have an alternative plan. The whitetails were useful to the fairies in many ways, mostly because they knew how to outwit men, and Scuri'Boo was reluctant to lose their company. On his way back from his meeting in Thistle Town with Barzad, he came upon Uulor, so they journeyed together.

'What has you up in daylight?' Scuri'Boo asked as he waved.

'Well, Scuri, as you know, I'm usually asleep at this time, but something is going on in Soggybog, and I feel I must go and see.'

'Not something bad, I hope?' Scuri'Boo's face had fallen.

'Oh, no. It's something wonderful, I'm sure.'

Scuri'Boo skipped in rings around Uulor in excitement, inwardly relieved that their common fear of men was not already a reality. Soon they found Kuz'Aar lying on the fence enjoying the heat of Golden Orb. He had lain down for a snooze as soon as he got away from Barzad. Kuz'Aar leapt up looking guilty. He expected that no one would be wandering this far from Thistle Town and that he could doze in peace. Seeing that it was only Scuri'Boo and Uulor, though, he relaxed, knowing he was in no trouble.

'Hard to get a rest round here,' he said, yawning. 'Barzad has me working . . .'

'Looks like that,' Uulor put in. 'What are you supposed to be doing?'

'I'm off to Soggybog to see this forest fairy Wui-bur brought home.'

Uulor and Scuri'Boo knew nothing of Fari-bur. Each had a purpose of his own in the marsh, so they made their slow, laborious way there together; Kuz'Aar was the only one with a seed, and his two companions made hard work of the journey, so, like a child on a bicycle with two friends on foot, Kuz'Aar stopped and started and eventually abandoned his seed.

The celebrations in Soggybog were in full swing. Vi'Shay and Bor'Tem were paddling by the banks of the bendy river, where the worship of buttercups was the main topic of conversation. Bor'Tem was fascinated by the marsh belief that buttercups would bring youth and intended to research it in detail. Stooping Reed awoke from his first sleep. Dun'Nuur and Dun'Mee were left to rest while all the fairies made their happy way, bringing the new-born with them, to the Bull-rush theatre to dance in rings and drink any nectar the bees had not taken to their hives earlier in the summer.

Wui-bur talked alone with Fari-bur while his many friends enjoyed the festivities. The talk was of Gloomy Forest and all the enchanting things that lived there. Many were curious to see the lone fairy, who knew all its creatures. She called them the 'night hosts'. Warmly, Wui-bur invited her to stay in Soggybog, where feather-bills and web-weavers were scarce and where the nectar of buttercups could be found in abundance. She accepted his invitation with enthusiasm and knew not that there was an ulterior motive behind it.

Golden Orb was low in the sky when the three wandering companions arrived, each on his own mission. Uulor was unable to contain himself by the time he reached the point where the marsh lay open and wide before him. To the gathering they went, and Stooping Reed was shown to him. A large circle was made as the fairies stepped back, giving them room. Some looked suspiciously at Uulor and whispered to their friends, 'What doom will he foretell now? Why has he come to dampen our party?'

Since they left on their long journey, many fairies were afraid of Uulor. He had led them safely to the lea, following only his instinct, and despite his obvious success, many seemed to forget Uulor's part in their salvation. He was misunderstood, and so he became more alone than ever, appearing only when necessary. He bore his solitude with the dignity of an elder, but Uulor never got used to loneliness. He spent his days asleep, for few would talk to him anyway. The nights were his alone to roam the lea, guarding his sleeping charges from any danger that may befall them. He saw many things on his lone wanderings and knew almost everything about everybody, from what they revealed in their sleep; and he must surely have wondered how the coming of Stooping Reed was not known to him before it occurred. Uulor's insight was slowly failing him, and the magic around him was waning, as with all his friends. They were tired from the journey, worried and unsure. Had Barzad understood this worry, he would have found the answer to the greyness that only he could see.

Kuz'Aar was anxious to find Bor'Tem quickly and return to Thistle Town, where Barzad would be waiting. He was late already with having to abandon his seed. Scuri'Boo knew the whitetails would also be waiting and was glad when they finally found her by the riverbank with Vi'Shay. They had a nutshell full of nectar, and both were showing signs of having drunk plenty already. White Orb[8] was due anytime, but the pair had no intentions of going to sleep. High-pitched laughter came from Bor'Tem, and she was dancing clumsily. Vi'Shay slipped off his

---

[8]     White orb—or white orb of the night is the moon

twig and plopped onto the mossy floor with his legs in the air. Kuz'Aar was beginning to like Soggybog.

The four stayed by the riverbank and drank by the light of White Orb for many hours. Kuz'Aar impersonated Barzad and made jokes at his expense. He was beginning to feel liberated. 'So what if I'm late.' he thought. 'Barzad can wait.' The birth of a new fairy was something to celebrate, indeed. It brought hope to the lea, for if a child could be born the long journey was not in vain, and other offspring might follow.

'It was good that Uulor came,' Vi'Shay pondered aloud. 'Perhaps the young ones would fear him less if he would only be more sociable.'

'I thought he might say something about those men the whitetails saw,' Scuri'Boo said.

'Did they really see men?' asked Kuz'Aar in a whisper.

'Who can say? But the whitetails know this land better than us, and we should heed their warnings.'

'More nectar, anyone?' sang Bor'Tem, determined to lighten the mood.

In the Bull-rush theatre, the celebrations were coming to an end. Tired fairies were meandering home to their beds in twos and threes. Dun'Nuur and Dun'Mee were fast asleep still, for the joy of the morning had worn them out. In Dandelion Village, Tu'Hob was preparing dandelion milk for the marshes in honour of the great day. Boo, the lone gossip had been to Soggybog earlier and brought the good news back to Inner Lea. The birth of a fairy so soon after the long journey was something to marvel at, and here at least, Uulor was quietly praised for his achievement in persuading them to follow him thus far.

By the brown fence in Windy Hill, the whitetails were huddled up in their warren deciding what to do if the threat of men should prove as serious as they feared. They knew not that Barzad was reluctant to help. They eagerly awaited Scuri'Boo, expecting him at any moment; they had been a long time and would do for long more.

And deep in the darkness of Thorny Tunnel, Barzad sat alone. Sleep had failed him all night. He must put on a happy face and wish Ben'Tork well on his move to Dandelion Village. He would see Ben'Tork again, he knew, but no joy was in him. He must wash and look good so that all the thistles would be pleased for Ben'Tork, his dear and trusted friend. The dandelions and thistles were leaving their beds, and the marshes were only now going. Today the news of Stooping Reed would spread throughout the lea, and all the fairies would know that the long journey had been worth it.

Bor'Tem and Scuri'Boo could find no way round Barzad's unwillingness to help the whitetails, and for them, this was most disappointing. Both could foresee problems, for the fairies remembered the kindness shown to them in Weedy Lea and were loath to embark on another long journey. Weedy Lea was big enough for fairies and whitetails—they just had to find a compromise somewhere. Kuz'Aar awoke and, finding a stray thistle seed, made his way back to Thistle Town, where Barzad would surely be waiting. To his surprise, Barzad said nothing of his late arrival and seemed distant. He stared blankly at the door when Kuz'Aar came in, and his gaze remained there a long time. Kuz'Aar guessed that Ben'Tork must have finally left, and he felt for Barzad in his sorrow.

'I found Bor'Tem, and she will have a report on Gloomy Forest for you soon.'

A pause followed, and then came a reaction from Barzad. 'Oh. I forgot about that.'

Kuz'Aar saw that Barzad was unhappy and felt guilty for cracking jokes the previous night. There came from within Barzad's chest the sigh of a weak and heartbroken fairy, and it made Kuz'Aar embarrassed.

'Have you had breakfast? I'll go and get you some.' He went outside and was glad to escape the awkwardness, but he came back quickly with petals and bark. Barzad hadn't moved, and a lone tear was sliding down his cheek.

'He'll be back.' Kuz'Aar tried to console him, but Barzad and Ben'Tork had been like brothers, and Kuz'Aar knew he would be sorely missed.

# Sprightly Go Lightly

Golden Orb rose and fell several times since that night when Barzad sat alone. He had not been seen much since Ben'Tork packed his things and brought them, bit by bit, to Dandelion Village: first his blade-whistle and then his council diaries, his leaf clothes, and, last but most important, a few trinkets given him by his thistle friends to remember them by. Eventually, he came back for a visit with his old friend, and Barzad awoke in Thorny Tunnel looking forward to the day. He had a stem-full of thistle nectar hidden out back, where Kuz'Aar couldn't find it. Since he appointed Kuz'Aar his helper, Barzad had more time to reflect on personal issues, namely Bur-duun. Kuz'Aar was not so happy with the arrangement, for he quite liked to be with her also, but he was too afraid to upset his grumpy chief. So every day Kuz'Aar went out to work while all his friends met and danced, rode the seed, sang, did all the things that fairies love, and he grew to resent Barzad's authority deeply.

By now Bur-duun had been in Thistle Town for a while and made many friends. Horaf and Shubar loved to ride the seed, bringing Bur-duun with them to Soggybog. Bor'Tem worked tirelessly there, researching buttercup worship and Gloomy Forest. Bur-duun was renowned for her beauty, and Bor'Tem was not lacking in charm either, though her talents were more of personality. She could make the night feel young, and for Bur-duun she was a good excuse to get away from Thistle Town and Barzad's constant gaze. She told Barzad she loved another fairy, but it made no difference; he craved her company, and when she was reluctant he nagged her for it. She feared to tell him who, lest Barzad become jealous of Kuz'Aar and make him work even harder, so they kept their love secret, and it took the good out of her move to Thistle Town.

But Barzad began to get annoyed by her constant trips to Soggybog; he wanted to spend time with her alone. She would not go to Soggybog so much if her sister were not there, he thought, so he sent Kuz'Aar to fetch Bor'Tem, saying he needed her report on Gloomy Forest. This destroyed Bur-duun and Kuz'Aar's hopes of catching some time together, and Kuz'Aar had little free time as it was, so they hid behind the tall grasses and conjured up an excuse for Bur-duun to go with him.

'Barzad must never know about us.' Kuz'Aar began. 'But you coming to Soggybog with me might look obvious.'

'Well, I can't say I want to see Bor'Tem again or he won't let me go, so let us pretend I need to see Scuri'Boo,' Bur-duun suggested.

'Yes. He's in the marsh now with Bor'Tem. They are discussing something to do with whitetails, I think. But why would you want to see him?'

'We could say he's teaching me to read the leaves.'

'Yes. That could work, but you hardly know Scuri'Boo.'

'No, but he and Bor'Tem are friends. I've often talked with him while she was with me. Surely it's not that inconceivable that I should know him.'

'OK, that's what we'll say.'

They parted with their plan hatched, and little did they know how it would backfire.

Alone later, Bur-duun knocked on his leaf door, and Barzad let her in. Finding room by moving aside all his odds and ends, he motioned her to be seated. He was by no means a house-proud fairy, so his home was looking dishevelled. Rather than make Thorny Tunnel decent for visitors, he would spend his time planning the future and thinking deep thoughts, so he was painfully unprepared for the guest sitting before him, with not even a place to sit but the mossy, damp floor, littered with the projects he was working on. Feeling uncomfortable already, she cut to the chase and asked to go to Soggybog, giving their little white lie as a reason. He happily granted her wish, glad to let his generosity show. She left him, laughing, and escaped unseen into the arms awaiting her where the tall grasses grew. Little did Barzad know how he had played into their hands, but as he thought of her, he began to see Scuri'Boo in a new light, and jealousy grew within him. He did not believe their excuse of reading the leaves. He believed it was just a lie to cover up their being together, which Bur-duun did not want known. Again he was alone. Feeling inspired now, he brought out his hazelnut guitar and put to music any words that sprang from the catacomb of his mind.

Fari-bur decided to live in the marsh and settled down with Wui-bur in Ferny Arch. She grew to love their ways and learned many marsh jigs. Often she would go to Gloomy Forest to feel again the magical thrill of shadows thrown, for she loved the mighty oaks and their deep shade. Sometimes a fairy or two would prance up beside her and stay for a while, hopping from one leg to the other in anticipation, like swallows gathering in preparation for their great journey south. Some would go to the forest with her, and they would dance and sing all night under the smiling white orb.

'Let us go to Gloomy Forest,' Fari-bur suggested just as Bur-duun and Kuz'Aar arrived. 'We can wait here for others to join.'

So Wui-bur waited by the barriers with Fari-bur, Scuri'Boo, and the three thistles, and soon there were many. Golden Orb was sinking, and some became anxious to set off; but Fari-bur stayed them. 'White Orb of the night is coming up. He is full and will give us enough light. We will wait.' So they waited, and when the moon was full and bright, they set off along the fence towards the shadows of Gloomy Forest.

The creatures of night were beginning to stir, but Fari-bur was not afraid, she knew them well. There was a squealing-four-legs[9] who would pretend to be in distress and capture any prey that came to his aid. There were furry-scurries[10] who burrowed into the ground and were eaten by the night-bills, and there were tree creatures[11] who ate nuts. Learned, the acorn, was watchful of them. Scuri'Boo thought he had seen one before and was not envious of acorns.

Soon they reached the edge of the lea, where the long grasses grew, and gathered themselves together.

'We must stay close,' Fari-bur advised, looking intently at each of her companions. There was Wui-bur and Vi'Shay, the eldest, for whom they had to stop often, as he could not keep up. He was reluctant at first, but when he saw that De'Lyza was going, he was glad. De'Lyza was Tu'Hob's aged brother and walked with a limp. Dun'Nuur and Dun'Mee brought young Stooping Reed, who was now so big that many plants bent under his weight. Gor'Teeb was a beautiful dandelion, a friend of the sisters Bor'Tem and Bur-duun. These three came also, and Scuri'Boo.

It was a long time before they were in the heart of the forest. By now they were used to the noises and were enjoying themselves immensely. White Orb had disappeared behind a cloud, and the forest floor was pitch dark, a beautiful, mysterious void of blindness.

'I'm pretty tired,' said De'Lyza, and he groped around, unsure of his footing, to find a tuft of moss to lie on. Vi'Shay followed suit, but everyone else was wide awake, so they got to work on the loose stones nearby, rolling them into a fairy ring. They sat around it, talking of the good times they remembered, and Barzad was not there to keep them from their ways of old.

---

9    A squealing-four-legs is a fox.

10   Furry-scurries are mice, rats, and other small rodents.

11   Tree creatures are usually squirrels.

A blade-whistle came out from under someone's arm, and a seed-drum was quickly made. There were dandelion poetry and marsh dances, and it was a magical night, deep in the forest under cover of darkness. They feasted on lichen and played hide-and-seek in the young saplings; and everywhere their graceful feet landed or their little hands touched, every dying twig and thirsty shoot was restored to life and grew proud and healthy long after the fairies had gone, for this was one night when their weariness was forgotten and the magic of their touch was restored.

When their party was over, the fairies slept where they fell, exhausted by the night of celebration. De'Lyza and Vi'Shay awoke late the following afternoon to find all their friends lying scattered around the fairy ring they had made.

'Looks like we missed quite a fete,' said Vi'Shay.

'No Barzad here to spoil the fun. Could be that the young ones will come here often.'

It was a while before the others awoke, and when they did it was time to go back to the lea. They knew where they were now, and Fari-bur had no need to lead them. They wandered off in twos and threes, talking amongst themselves of their adventure. Fari-bur stayed behind, reluctant to return just yet. Her friends reached the lea long before Golden Orb fell and were greeted by many. Tu'Hob welcomed the elderly De'Lyza with the eagerness of familial love. A great feast was held where Thistle Town meets the marsh, using the bounty they brought back. There were nuts, nectar, and delicious campion seeds. The belle of the ball was Bor'Tem. All the attention was hers because she was leaving for Thistle Town in the morning. Everyone wished her well and hoped she would return soon to continue her great work on buttercup worship. Stooping Reed especially would miss her, for they had grown close and she was like a second mother to him, teaching him many things a fairy of his tender age would not normally know.

Barzad was there too, hiding behind the stem of a nettle. He had learned of the trip to the forest, and now his fear of shame was doubled. What if all the fairies should discover his terror of Gloomy Forest? He would be a laughing stock. Best to feign disinterest, he decided, but his curiosity got the better of him, and he could not keep away. He looked on sternly, but secretly he was glad they had all made it safely back. The thought of losing a fairy to such a dark place instilled fear enough to drag his heart out through his mouth.

Kuz'Aar trod home during the night. Fear of Barzad pulled him faster than his legs would normally drag him, but he could not find Barzad in Thorny Tunnel or anywhere in Thistle Town. He thought about returning to share the fun, knowing that having tried to find Barzad, he would be in no trouble, but instead, he went to his makeshift hut and curled up to sleep. There he remained while his friends enjoyed the party, but had he known that Barzad was there all along, where Bur-duun danced and sang, his resentment of Barzad would have found new depths.

Evening had come quickly to Gloomy Forest, and for the first time Fari-bur felt uneasy. She was alone now, with the voices of her friends ringing in her ears against the unusual silence of the forest, not normally so still. She found a cosy tuft of moss and sat on it, listening for familiar sounds. A squealing-four-legs was out of his den and looked intently at her for a while. It was a young four-legs and had never seen a fairy before; he looked again and walked away. It was then that she felt the presence of another fairy.

Not far away, between the leaves of a sapling, she could see the gaunt little face of Uulor, lonest of all fairies. Not many knew him, but Fari-bur recognised the pale, wizened old face her father had talked of when she was growing up. Even during the long journey, he went ahead, searching the way, feeling his direction, lest he should lead them into a danger he had not anticipated. Many travelled that journey, not knowing who they were following and never seeing him who led the way. Even when Stooping Reed arrived and Uulor came to the marsh, she was away with Wui-bur and escaped the uneasiness of his presence. She knew him only as Uulor the lone, who came out at night bringing with him great change, and he was far less famous for leading them to their safe haven than he was infamous for his dark tales of men.

'You must not be alone, Fari-bur,' Uulor whispered hoarsely. 'You need your mate with you at a time like this.' And he turned away, fading into the greyness of falling fog.

She was bewildered. Scared and shaking, she wandered back to the lea that dark and cloudy night, and she didn't notice the many pink faces of forest blossoms awaken and look towards her, reflecting the light of Golden Orb though the night had come. A wonderful thing was happening to Fari-bur, and she knew nothing of it. But the night hosts saw something different about her, and two young owls hooted loudly with unmistakable glee. Uulor slipped away to his hidden home, and he understood her coming joy.

It was very late when her feet felt the damp of marsh. Most were asleep after their fete, but Vi'Shay and a few others were still awake, so she told them of her encounter with Uulor, hoping for something encouraging.

'Uulor, lonest of all fairies,' said Vi'Shay. 'He did not seek you in Gloomy Forest for a trifle. Something very important will happen.' A silence fell upon the fairies.

'"You need your mate with you at a time like this." Those were his exact words,' said Fari-bur, her little lips wobbling and her eyes ready for tears.

'Maybe he put a spell on you!' Stooping Reed thought aloud and was given a sharp dig for his indiscretion.

'Nonsense! Stooping Reed, go to your bed.' Dun-Mee was a firm mother.

'But he has magic powers,' came from someone else.

'No fairy has magic powers,' joined Ben'Tork, who had come from Dandelion Village. 'He is wise, and we should be grateful to have him. Was it not he who led us from fear and unrest to the safety of Weedy Lea?'

With that, another silence fell upon the fairies—this one more hopeful. Fari-bur was exhausted, so she went away slowly to sleep on a buttercup.

'She'll be all right,' Ben'Tork assured them. 'Now! Has anyone seen Bor'Tem?'

Bor'Tem was finishing the notes in her diary. Her council duties were taking over, and Barzad would be displeased if he knew. But she would soon be finished with a lengthy account of Wui-bur's trip to Gloomy Forest and of the birth of Stooping Reed. Secretly, she looked forward to the day when she would sit alone with him in Thorny Tunnel telling him many things he did not know. He would take her seriously then; he would listen to her and perhaps develop a regard for her as she had done for him.

Dun'Mee led Ben'Tork to her patch, and soon all talk of Fari-bur and Gloomy Forest was at an end. The tired fairies went their separate ways for the night. Ben'Tork, Bor'Tem, Dun'Mee, and Dun'Nur stayed awake and spent the night dancing marsh reels and reciting the poetry of dandelions. It was a beautiful, peaceful night, and they were still awake when Golden Orb arose from behind Windy Hill, her happy, yellow sparkles twinkling all across the marsh dampness.

Some awoke and talked quietly among themselves, but soon the whole marsh was a-whisper. Another fairy had been born in the night, and the lucky mother was Fari-bur, who awoke to find her tiny offspring dancing on the dewy petals. A lively daughter it was. Cause for celebration, indeed! They named her 'Sprightly-go-lightly' on account of her obvious love of dance. Sprightly would occasionally stop dancing to stare intently at Golden Orb and then at the buttercups. Her parents saw that she loved the yellow of the morning and dressed her in a buttercup petal tied together with blades of grass. They brought her to the middle of the marsh to show her off, and the marshes celebrated with the custom of their race. Dun'Nur and Dun'Mee were there. They showed her to Stooping Reed, and instantly he loved her. Wui-bur saw this and smiled inwardly. It was very soon, but as the custom of fairies went, children grew to adulthood quickly and were slow to mature thereafter, so it was normal for fairies to form a union at an early age.

# MANY OFFSPRING

The season of thistles was long and eventful that first autumn in Weedy Lea, and then came the cold winter. Frosty nights, and the ponds froze over, but the fairies didn't mind. The marsh fairies had discovered skating, fun and athletic. Bor'Tem described it to all she knew. Even Barzad was impressed, but still he preferred the thistle way of riding the seed. Sometimes a stray seed would be discovered by the odd, lucky fairy, who would ride high where all could see, squealing gleefully. Horaf and Shubar both found seeds, and they knew a way to tie theirs down, preventing them from blowing away. They showed Barzad in the hope of getting him to ride outside Thistle Town; Barzad had rarely been away from Thistle Town since they first settled, and now, when others talked of Soggybog, he realized that he had been missing out. He really must let Ben'Tork bring him some day.

'Later, maybe, when the seeds are back,' he thought, for Ben'Tork was without.

Uulor had not been seen since his trip to Gloomy Forest, but Scuri'Boo knew where he lived. He made his secret den far from the village clusters, at the foot of Windy Hill, where Golden Orb seldom shone her rays. Dark and dreary was his home—hidden, cold, and lonely. He rarely went to Soggybog, where laughter was heard and friends pulled each other along on sleds made of fallen leaves. He had worries. To the other fairies, the long journey had paid off. There were offspring, and many more might follow. But Uulor knew it was not that simple, as did Scuri'Boo and the whitetails. He had been watching for men since first they were seen at the warren. Bor'Tem could find no way to help them, so she and Scuri'Boo held a council meeting, together, to find a solution.

'Barzad is going to disapprove no matter where they dig.'

'You're right, Bor'Tem. But how can the whitetails get beyond him?' Scuri'Boo sat with his head in his hands and his elbows on his knees. Frustration clearly showed on his face. frustration at Barzad, who seemed to forget this land belonged not to the fairies but to the whitetails and high weeds who gave willingly and received little in return.

Bor'Tem echoed his thoughts. 'If anything, it is us fairies who should move. The whitetails and high weeds may tire of giving all the time. Wui-bur is convinced we should not ride the seed, yet we thistles still do so when we can. What if the weeds get angry? They might put a spell on us.'

'And the whitetails could set a trap for us. If they can outsmart men, they can outsmart us. We must let them build where they want, and Barzad may learn to like it.'

Having made their decision, the two separated. Bor'Tem started straight for Thorny Tunnel, quietly anticipating an evening with Barzad. She would not tell him about their council decision—Scuri'Boo would do that later. Instead, she would tell him all she knew of Gloomy Forest and Fari-bur; this would impress him and soften his heart towards her.

Ben'Tork went to visit Tork, his mother. Tu'Hob and she were old friends, closer than many knew, and the two looked forward to an afternoon of hilarity with Ben'Tork. 'Gentle son of Tork'—they named him well. Ben'Tork had no business living in Thistle Town with his feisty friend Barzad; a bad influence when they were children, and holding him back as an adult. Tork was relieved to see them separated, though she loved dark Barzad as her own.

Tu'Hob had a stem-full of nettle nectar. He always knew how to harvest the plant juices, even in the thirsty winters.

Tork was glad he had no council duties today. Ben'Tork played blade-whistle and wobbled his legs that funny way while she and Tu'Hob danced. Evening stretched into night. Ben'Tork talked of Thistle Town, describing how lovely the sparkling fires[12] were, when seen from the swaying thistle heights and the fun he had with Barzad when it was just the two of them, with no issues and no politics. Ben'Tork and Tork were smiling, and Tu'Hob felt a sadness that he could not relate to Barzad, though he tried so hard. And he wished he could make Barzad understand all the good the fairy council could do. Barzad's strength and influence would be great for the council, but it would not be.

Dun'Nur and Dun'Mee held a dinner party for their leader and his new spouse. Talk was slow, with just a few passing comments, while all four gazed at the children: the handsome, athletic Stooping Reed and the delicate, dancing Sprightly-go-lightly. All that existed for Wui-bur were Fari-bur and the two laughing children on the floor; it occurred to him that Stooping Reed would win many hearts, though his own was pledged already.

The marshes were first to have fairy children, but they were not the last. Many followed, and next to be blessed were Horaf and Shubar. Having played and laughed and eaten and sung together, they went to sleep and awoke the following morning with their ears being pulled. Grass Venture had come into the world, first of the thistle babies, and dragged his bewildered parents outside to go exploring. They took him to a seed, and he was not long learning to ride. They followed him, protecting his tiny body from thorns, and brought him to Thorny Tunnel, where their friend and leader lived. Barzad awoke wondering

---

[12] Sparkling fires are stars, planets, galaxies, or any other celestial object that reflects or emits light, except for the sun and moon (which are Golden Orb and White Orb). When fairies refer to the sparkling fires, it is usually stars they mean.

at all the noise, and looked outside to see the two riding high above the peaks with Grass Venture between them. Joy had come to Thistle Town, and Barzad wasted no time. He blew loudly through his stem-horn, and instantly all the thistles were awake.

As Horaf and Shubar bobbed up and down on their seeds a thought came to Barzad. When he first rode a seed, after Uulor found the lea, Horaf and Shubar were next to try. Now the youth of their making could not be got down. Grass Venture bounced to and fro dangerously, but he had mastered the art already.

Barzad threw a feast. A stem-full of nectar was brought out, and many more followed. Dandelions weren't long hearing the news. Boo was up already making her rounds of the lea, and she told De'Lyza when they met for their usual morning wash. Tu'Hob finally had his chance to talk to Barzad without political barriers between them. His family left their own party, which lasted through the night, and headed straight to Thistle Town with a net full of nettle needles. Tu'Hob knocked on Barzad's door.

'Here is a gift to celebrate Thistle joy.' Tu'Hob presented the nettle needles Tork had cooked. Barzad threw open the door, and the three entered. Ben'Tork and Barzad skipped in rings when they met. Little had either known, when last they parted, that they would meet again so soon or so happily.

The party lasted many hours. Barzad's home was deceptively large, and the fairies were not cramped. He had tidied up since Bur-duun paid her last visit, and now Thorny Tunnel looked bright and cheerful. Bor'Tem arrived from Soggybog, Ben'Tork played his blade-whistle, some maracas were made of dried seeds, and Gor'Teeb sang till Golden Orb fell to her unknown hiding place behind the world. High above, the sparkling fires twinkled in shades of white and yellow and blue, crisp with the winter chill, some rising, some setting, spinning circles in the sky. A few wispy clouds rode by, hiding the constellations in their muslin curtains, but Orion was too enormous, so Betelgeuse and Rigel pierced through the leaves of Thistle Town. Eventually only Bor'Tem remained. Finally she had Barzad cornered in his own home. Now she could talk, and he would listen. The stem-juice was all gone, but so what? They were alone. He listened while she told him of all the wonders of Soggybog and of the buttercup worship that made the fairies happy, having something to believe in. She told him of Stooping Reed's devotion to the buttercups, how lovely they were to sleep in, and how bright they made the morning. She described the frozen ponds where the fairies skated, the beautiful icicles, dripping as they thawed, and the fabulous Fari-bur, who showed them the ways of Gloomy Forest. Here he began to fidget so that she would not detect his fear of Gloomy Forest, but she misread his nervousness as boredom and was sorely wounded.

Soon after, one sunny, frost-free morning, she and Bur-duun went to visit their parents, Arthos and Tem. They were a lively pair; thistle life suited them well. Why their daughters followed them to Thistle Town, Barzad could not understand; clearly Bor'Tem preferred the marsh, and before coming to Thistle Town Bur-duun had chosen a lone life. Barzad was inwardly joyous when she first came to Thistle Town, but his joy was soon dampened when she shunned his attention and stamped on his heart. Bor'Tem arrived first and climbed up the familiar nettle stem to her parents' hut, high among the new shoots. The hut was built, like a bird's nest, of twigs and clay; rain freely pooled on their musty floor. Neither were bothered by this glaring inconvenience—Tem loved to follow the rain, and Arthos loved to follow Tem.

The two were sitting with their legs stretched out, relaxed and half asleep, when Bor'Tem peeped over their twig and clay wall.

'Hullo.'

'Ah! You're here! And where is your sister?'

'Gor'Teeb has her. They're putting petals in her hair,' she said, climbing inside.

Arthos brought out a basket of tasty buds, and Tem made space so she could sit between them.

'We've just been to Inner Lea. Ben'Tork was there—'

'He's really enjoying Dandelion Village,' Tem interrupted. 'Hope you'll keep in touch with him. It's not so far away as the marsh, you know.'

Tem had always believed Ben'Tork and Bor'Tem would become mates. They had been friends since childhood and were similar in personality. No party was whole without Bor'Tem's stories and Ben'Tork's music, and together they made the perfect pair, but there was only the love of friends between them.

Bur-duun arrived, groomed and beautiful. Her parents made the usual fuss.

'Oh, look at your hair! Isn't she lovely?'

'Fabulous! Gorgeous.' They both rose again for a nutshell of rainwater and more buds.

Bor'Tem pulled out her new blade-whistle and played a few inferior bars of a well-known jig. Bur-duun, still standing, began to dance, and the party had started. For Bur-duun this was what Thistle Town was all about: visiting her family and dancing to music. She did her best to get into the humour, but her parents were concerned. They could see that the beautiful Bur-duun was not herself. Had they known chief, Barzad, was behind her troubles, they would have eased her mind. She told them nothing of his attentions or of Kuz'Aar, who possessed her heart, for their love was secret. The party drew to a close late in the afternoon, but another was starting in Inner Lea. Peeping Bud had arrived, and none knew who her parents were. When the dandelions awoke, she was already hiding in the spring shoots. She was shown to her leader. Tu'Hob could not find among them any face that hers resembled, but she was not parentless, for all Inner Lea were her guardians and it was quite normal for fairies to be born in this way.

Scuri'Boo knew nothing of the new fairies in Thistle Town and Inner Lea; he knew only that many more whitetails were coming, and the does would be anxious to dig. It was decided that a new warren would begin, and so Scuri'Boo made the journey to Thistle Town, where he must persuade Barzad that the fairies would not be affected. The recent joy of Thistle Town did nothing to soften Barzad towards the news, and he was no lover of compromise. It took all of Scuri'Boo's diplomatic skills to keep him calm. As he was leaving Thistle Town, having saved the whitetails from certain discovery by men, instead of exhilaration Scuri'Boo felt only banishment and failure. Barzad showered upon him a tirade of abuse that lasted many hours, naming him a traitor to the fairies, a puppet for the whitetails, and many other things, leaving Scuri'Boo too humbled even to defend himself. To Scuri'Boo, Barzad seemed crazed beyond redemption, too angry and arrogant to listen to his explanation. To Barzad, Scuri'Boo was the secret lover Bur-duun would not reveal, so he vented his jealousy on the unfortunate lone before him. In the heat of his wrath, Barzad had entirely forgotten to tell Scuri'Boo that Grass Venture had come into the world.

Now all but the lones had fairy children to love. In the marsh were Stooping Reed, first of the babies, and Sprightly-go-lightly, dancing jewel of the ponds. Later there was Hazy Mellow, who came after a lengthy feast where copious amounts of stem juice had been drunk. Hazy was intoxicated when first he was discovered, hence the name. He knew not who his parents were, but, like Peeping Bud, he was guarded by all. Of the Dandelions there was Peeping Bud, adept in the art of camouflage. Dandelion Dew and Daisy Petal were later, twin daughters of Sula'Tan and Tuss'Kazuu. High Wind followed later. Soft and meek, he was the very image of his race, but he hardly knew the cushioned life led by most dandelions until he conquered his struggle with Barzad. Grass Venture was the first born in Thistle Town. After his appearance, there was a lull during which few were born, but still they came, individually and at intervals. Their coming was celebrated with less vigour, for the fairies already knew they were saved; the long journey had been successful, and that was most important, no matter how joyous the occasion of a new arrival.

Hazy Mellow spoke in musical tones and was never far from Stooping Reed, who likewise was never far from Sprightly-go-lightly, she being the sunshine of his day. The three marsh fairies were close friends, and there was much laughter and sport between them. Grass Venture came often to visit, and they played by the reed huts in the morning, where Vi'Shay liked to wash. The highlight of his day was when he saw the beautiful children at their games. Stooping Reed and Grass Venture shared a bond unlike the friendship of most children. Grass Venture understood from an early age the ways of the lea, and he was kind to little Sprightly, of whom Stooping Reed was enormously protective. He played with Sprightly when Stooping Reed was busy with Bor'Tem, studying the buttercups. Now that Bor'Tem was back in Thistle Town, Stooping Reed had a lot to do alone, so he was glad that Grass Venture played with her often and brought her exploring, where she learned many nice things.

Bor'Tem and Bur-duun met one morning to practice spells, but none would work, so they parted ways. Bor'Tem went off to central Thistle Town, where her home was surrounded by many, and Bur-duun to the outskirts, where her nettle-hut lay hidden, alone and undisturbed. When she arrived at her hut, Bur-duun was surprised to find Barzad waiting by the leaf door.

After Scuri'Boo had gone, Barzad sat alone thinking to himself that he was wrong to argue with Scuri'Boo as he had done. Scuri'Boo was right about the whitetails; Barzad knew that, so why create awkwardness where none existed? That would give Bur-duun another reason to despise him, and she had enough of those already.

In his remorse he decided to send Scuri'Boo to help the whitetails build their new warren, but Scuri'Boo would not approach him again. So Barzad set off to find another who would give the message and who better than Bur-duun? He waited by her little nettle-hut all day, nervous but happy, until finally she arrived and found him there. Clearly she did not expect him, and her reaction told instantly of shock, which she tried to disguise as surprise.

'Lovely afternoon! How are your parents?' Barzad began as kindly as he could, not noticing his glaring omission of Bor'Tem.

'If I knew I'd be having a visitor, I would have come earlier.'

'Good. I'm glad you didn't, then!'

Inside her hut, Bur-duun produced a pouch of nettle needles Tem had given her to take home and placed them on the floor. Barzad tucked into them straight away. He missed breakfast in his rush to set things straight with Scuri'Boo and had nothing to eat during his long wait for Bur-duun. She presented some water, and they ate silently for a while.

'Well! No doubt you're wondering why I'm here. This is not a social call, you know.'

'It isn't?'

'No. I'm sure you've been talking to Scuri'Boo since his visit to Thistle Town.'

'No. Was I supposed to? I didn't even know he was here.'

Barzad laughed, taking her words as a little white lie. 'You don't have to pretend. I think Scuri'Boo is right. We need to get moving quickly to be in time for the new whitetails.'

'Why? What are we doing?'

'You and Scuri'Boo are going to the whitetails, and neither of you will come back until their new city is built.' Barzad was laughing. He thought he was giving her a gift; and little did he know the error he was making.

She thought of the whitetails building a city underground, in the skull of the earth. What could two fairies do that would be of any use to them? She thought of the torturously long time away from Kuz'Aar and of Barzad, who laughed as he sent her away from her friends, with only the lone fairy Scuri'Boo for company. Sullenly, she went to find Scuri'Boo and as her dislike of Barzad grew to hatred, she little knew her own error.

# THE WHITETAIL CITY

Golden Orb began to rise. Inner Lea was quiet, with the peaceful calm enjoyed only by those without a care. Sula'Tan and Tuss'Kazuu lay where the cowslips would soon be in bloom, for spring had come at last. Safe and snug between them were the girls, Dandelion Dew and Daisy Petal, all breathing softly in deep sleep. Soggybog in the west, where Golden Orb rose from the night void, waited for the day; a plop and splash told of early risers such as Vi'Shay and Wui-bur grooming blindly in dark ponds. Daisies on tiny stems crouched near the barriers at Gloomy Forest, droopy and dull in the dawn half-light. Scuri'Boo lay curled up asleep beneath the barrier where Windy Hill towers over the lea, and not far away in Thistle Town, Bur-duun slept the fitful sleep of one greatly unhappy—Kuz'Aar, awake beside her. Bor'Tem usually came for breakfast, and it was nearly time. He snuck out carefully, so as not to wake Bur-duun, slipped down the long stem, and silently stole away before anyone saw. Golden Orb was almost over the lea. Her light was enough for Kuz'Aar to see by, and as he crept through the blades of grass like a thief in the night, he saw Bor'Tem singing quietly to the lush green. She did not notice Kuz'Aar watching her, hiding, as she climbed up to the hut. Bor'Tem was deeply offended by Barzad. She had no idea, of course, that his treatment of her sister was even worse. Both saw only the bad in him, not the misunderstanding or their own part in it.

Arthos and Tem had always shared a high opinion of Barzad, but they could not understand what motive lay behind his sending Bur-duun to Whitetail City for no one knew how long. It was obvious now that Chief Barzad was behind Bur-duun's lack of spirit of late, but what occurred between them neither could guess.

During the morning, Grass Venture found Bor'Tem with her parents and persuaded them to go to Soggybog, and the four set out having nourished themselves. Bur-duun went off to find Scuri'Boo and hopefully catch a secret moment with Kuz'Aar. The entire family left Thistle Town, thinking they would never return. Grass Venture would find Sprightly-go-lightly, his favourite girl, and Hazy Mellow would show him how to extract juice from bog plants. Arthos and Tem looked forward to meeting Fari-bur for the first time. In the fresh, pleasant breeze they soon put aside their hurt with the help of the young thistle boy, who sang and talked and lifted the mood.

As the last light faded, the grass beneath their feet grew sparse and wet, until the marsh lay before them. Hazy Mellow greeted them, clearly inebriated, having drunk any sap he could get. They wandered on, leaving him to his smiling daze, and reached the bulrush theatre where the marshes often gathered to tell stories and sing. Mildly embarrassed at having brought nothing, they sat and shared news with their friends, politely declining any food offered, but to Wui-bur, their hunger was obvious.

'We would not let you starve after your journey. Tuck in,' he said, producing a reed-basket of leaf biscuits and leaving it within their reach.

In Thorny Tunnel, Barzad rearranged his notes and projects into some sort of order. Kuz'Aar had done a very poor job of filing, and now he had disappeared for the day. Barzad didn't mind. He was in no mood for company anyway since he sent Bur-duun away, and while he tidied his work, she and Scuri'Boo were leaving the last thistles behind them, facing the long stretch of grass to Inner Lea. There they said goodbye to Kuz'Aar, who shared the first steps of their journey. Leaving him alone between the towns, they continued to Dandelion Village while he returned home. Gor'Teeb played alone on the wide leaves of daisies. The fresh, fertile air smelt of spring. Daisies were blooming, dandelions would soon be yellow, and Gor'Teeb bounced, trampoline-like, on the flat leaves she loved so well. Scuri'Boo and Bur-duun joined her, and they shared news in the afternoon warmth and played together as they journeyed, Gor'Teeb relieving them of their low spirits in the way that Grass Venture was doing on the far side of the lea, asking many questions, singing, dancing, and running on ahead.

When Sprightly heard visitors had come to the marsh, she was eager to perform an amazing show for those gathered. The stage was set, and musicians produced their instruments. Hazy Mellow was charged with beverage duties—if he could be found. Bor'Tem offered her help in searching, a knowing smile hidden behind her hands. Arthos joined her in retracing their steps until they found him lying over a twig, arms outstretched, gazing at the sparkling fires. Hauling him to his feet was no easy task.

'The sky is beau-ti-ful.'

'Okay, Hazy.'

'Beauu-ti-ful.'

'They're having a party, Hazy. Can you find us more nectar or stem juice?'

'Ummh?'

'Everyone says you can find some. Don't they, Bor'Tem?'

'Oh, yea.' Bor'Tem looked unconvinced.

'I'll find it,' Hazy slurred. 'I'm the one for the shjob.'

Stooping Reed met them while his marsh friends danced, and together they looked for a suitable bog plant where copious amounts of stem juice could be found.

'We need lots, Hazy. Where's the best place?'

Hazy pointed vaguely and wobbled towards the bull rushes. Stooping Reed followed, but in the dark he stumbled and broke a stem, snapping it at the base. Precious sap began to ooze from the long hollow, but Hazy, thinking quickly for the first time in his life, slumped clumsily onto the reed's tip so the juice flowed downwards and could not escape. Deftly, Stooping Reed gathered up the length of reed and made for home, dragging the open base on his shoulders. Hazy followed behind, keeping the closed tip on the ground, until they heard the nearby hum of many voices singing in unison. The gathered crowd cried out in joyous triumph as the young ones placed their bounty in their midst. Thereafter, Hazy was recognised not as the boy who was always drunk but as the architect who designed the biggest stem juice pipe of all, and from that day forward, juices were had in plentiful supply for all occasions.

Hazy Mellow relished in his newfound importance. The thought of the way fairy girls would speak his name made his small chest fill with pride, but he knew Stooping Reed had played no small part in his discovery, and if Hazy Mellow could think of a subtle way to make that known to Sprightly-go-lightly, he surely would because, though they never talked of it, Hazy was not so slow as to miss his friend's love for her, nor was Grass Venture. Stooping Reed was full of strength and charisma one minute; the next, when Sprightly arrived, he was silent and mindful of himself. Grass Venture saw that making himself scarce would facilitate Stooping Reed's attempt to woo Sprightly, so he pretended to miss his parents, even though he had just arrived. Some elder fairies protested at him heading home alone in the dark.

'What will Thistle Town think of us if we send him home unguided?' This came from Fari-bur, and though Bor'Tem and her family were still sore with Barzad, they agreed. But when Vi'Shay spoke, everyone listened.

'The boy'll be fine. His parents didn't name him Grass Venture without reason. He'll be home before the rest of us are in bed.'

White Orb was young when Scuri'Boo and Bur-duun reached the part of land, just beyond the lea, where the whitetail city began. Gor'Teeb shared their journey to the long hedgerow. Then she went to find Uulor, who would be about, night having fallen. Unlike her friends, Gor'Teeb was not afraid of Uulor; she understood his feelings, knew his loneliness must hurt deeply, and sought to share her company with him. Scuri'Boo told her the way, so she found his dark home easily despite its hidden state. Drawing close to the little entrance, she heard a voice that was not Uulor's, and it puzzled her. It seemed she was not the only one who felt his loneliness, but who was the other? Creeping to the door, she recognised the gentle little voice of Boo, whispering things that made him laugh. Rather than make her presence known, Gor'Teeb slipped away, confused, as though from some embarrassing secret she should not have known.

She knew that Scuri'Boo and Bur-duun would be far away now, so she trod the dark way softly, and for the first time in her life, she felt truly alone. It occurred to her that perhaps Uulor was not 'the lonest of all fairies,' as is written in fairy lore; perhaps it was she, who walked all the night unaided, quickly getting lost. Often, Gor'Teeb wondered when she would find a mate. Her friends had settled, some had children, but she was still alone so now she wondered, 'Am I the lonest of us all?'

But she was not. And neither was Kuz'Aar, though he would disagree. He too walked alone, and his way was hard to find in the moonless dark, for clouds often obscured the light of White Orb. Bereft of his mate for he knew not how long, returning to work for Chief Barzad, whom he had come to despise, in Thistle Town where the glory that once attracted him had all but faded. Kuz'Aar knew of only one reason to go home at all, to be there some distant day when Bur-duun returned; so he, too, wondered, 'Am I the lonest of us all?' But he was not.

Nor was it the latest fairy child, born in no-man's-land without a parent to guide her, negotiating the tricky dark when all the orbs had voided themselves. The spring mists, the first mists she had ever known, shrouded her tiny face as she rode a damp seed through the thick air, instinct leading her to Thistle Town.

And far away in the pasture beyond the wooden fence, deep in their tunnels the whitetails were asleep. Scuri'Boo and Bur-duun allowed their feet to make some little noise, and those they woke led them to their chief. Big Buck breathed heavily in his sleeping trance, but it was not long before his chamber was filled with the quiet murmur of late-night talk. Tomorrow the arduous work would begin. The does were anxious to get started, and with Barzad's blessing they would dig to their hearts' content.

Later in the week, Golden Orb arose and made the morning warm. Barzad lay deep in thought, surrounded by the sleeping multitude of Thistle Town. Many questions were running through his mind. How long before Bur-duun would return? How would she act towards him? How would the other fairies react when she and Scuri'Boo announced their union? Surely they would understand his decision to send them away together. He must wait and see. He washed and dressed, rummaged through his neglected projects, laid them on the floor, and then rearranged them in order of preference. He did this several times, his concentration being poor and to add to the difficulty, the other fairies were awake and making a lot of noise outside. Finally, his concentration escaped him fully, so he opened his sharp and thorny door to see what all the fuss was about.

All the thistles had gathered and were standing in a ring around the mysterious fairy girl who wandered there, holding the fluttering seed on which she rode. No fairy among them knew who could be her parents, for she was different in some way, though no one could see how. Her seed, too, was different in a way the thistles could not know, for it was the seed of a dandelion. Joy had come again to Thistle Town, mixed with confusion.

'Grass Venture will be most pleased,' Horaf whispered quietly to his mate. It was intended as a joke, and Shubar took it as one. But Barzad heard the comment, and it made him glad, because secretly he agreed. It was a bone of contention for Barzad that Grass Venture should want to spend so much time in Soggybog, and despite Horaf and Shubar's approval, Barzad was worried he may be spending too much time with Sprightly-go-lightly; a nice fairy girl, no doubt, but a marsh all the same. A thistle beauty would suit him far better. Now there was one. From nearby, Ghenthem, Horaf's father, pulled out a rustic instrument made from bark and seeds, and soon he was surrounded by a large ring of fairies holding hands and dancing round him. Barzad couldn't help but notice the absence of Ben'Tork and his blade whistle. Someone asked aloud where Bor'Tem and her family were. At this, Barzad became thoughtful and silent, realising he had not seen any of them for days and never even missed them. That was a terrible mistake. He realised with a shock that they must have been aggrieved and left Thistle Town for good.

# DANDELION SEEDS

Tu'Hob awoke to the scent of spring flowers. Insects were busy, small feather-bills were chirping, and a gentle breeze stirred the whispering grass. He washed in the early dew and looked around. It was a strange morning; a thrill was in the air, so he wandered out to see what was new. Many had woken early, and most were conscious of the feeling he described, so it was not long before many had gathered in silent procession. During the past few weeks, there grew within Tu'Hob some anticipation he could not understand. As nature emerged from winter, colour came with it, but not the colour of spring he knew from years before or the bright skies of summer. This was something else. Instinct led Tu'Hob through the fragrant blooms and around the larger clumps of grass to a tiny mound where many dandelions grew. Here the fairies stopped and looked silently for a while, not understanding, at the perfectly spherical fluffy ball of a dandelion gone to seed. A low mumble began at the front of the crowd and progressed towards those farther back, growing in waves until everyone was talking freely and excitedly. As the pitch of talk rose, so too did the breeze, bringing with it a single seed from the abundant head. It fluttered for a few seconds, suspended in the scented air, and in a moment it was gone. A second of silence was followed by a stadium cheer as the fairies recognised at last. Joy had come again to Dandelion Village, whose greatness could not be denied, and the lives of dandelion fairies changed forever by their weed hosts. Just like the thistle fairies, those who chose to ride the seed could ride all summer long. Dandelions were everywhere. Seeds would be abundant. Tu'Hob laughed softly to himself as he thought in a rare moment of pride, *Barzad will be furious.*

And while the wildest party of Inner Lea got underway, gentle whispers were evidence of the work of whitetail does. Long into the day they were busy while the useless bucks looked on, ashamed of their ineptitude. In their midst Bur-duun and Scuri'Boo shuffled through notes and leaf maps, rustic scratchings pencilled in with thorns. Fairy food was scarce; there were only the grass and vegetables that whitetails gathered, which fairies wouldn't normally eat. Scuri'Boo went out early every morning in search of seeds and buds small enough to eat, and by the time he came back he was already tired. He longed to be back at the lea and quietly cursed Chief Barzad for sending him there. 'Who is Barzad to send me to the ends of the lea and beyond?' he thought aloud. 'Barzad is no chief of mine.'

He hated having to go out and forage in the unfamiliar territory of Whitetail City, and it occurred to him, not happily, that he and Bur-duun were the first fairies to venture so far beyond the barriers since the long journey. Beyond the barriers was no place for a fairy. Windy Hill, Whitetail City, even the pasture where enormous four-legs grazed—that land was the void, the *unlea.*

During the long time Bur-duun and Scuri'Boo spent away, many changes occurred in the lea. Arthos Tem and Bor'Tem settled comfortably in Soggybog. Tem loved the rain-spattered pools. Arthos followed her in the mornings to Vi'Shay's favourite place, and the three washed together often. Bor'Tem tried to forget her disappointment in Barzad and quickly got to work with Stooping Reed, researching buttercups. Fari-bur helped when she could, and her company was fresh in the long days of tired research. With the coming burst of buttercup growth, the workload was huge. The two were overloaded with leaves to examine. Bor'Tem was glad to be back, but she missed Barzad. Cruel as he was, he was her chief—her king. Wui-bur gladly welcomed the family, and after they had tried out all the places, he helped them find nice patches on which to live.

'You'll come and live near Ferny Arch, Bor'Tem?'

'I'll live wherever you like,' was her reply.

'Excellent. I'm not very experienced, you see. A young fairy like me could use your expertise.'

'You seem to be doing a good job so far. The marshes are happy and healthy.'

'Well . . . You see . . . I'm a bit worried about Vi'Shay.' Wui-bur became quiet. Bor'Tem patiently waited for him to start again.

'Since the long journey, he has been so weary. He was gaining strength there for a while, but his improvement has stalled somewhat. I think the cold winter hasn't helped.'

He went silent again.

'I see,' said Bor'Tem at last. 'Perhaps these rumours of men have him worried.'

'Vi'Shay doesn't believe in men. In his long life he has never seen a man once. Maybe they don't exist at all?'

'But Uulor says they were beside the whitetail city.'

'Uulor says lots of things, but are they all true? Two winters ago, before the long journey, he said the great feather-bills[13] were coming.'

'Maybe they came this winter. We're not there anymore, so how can we know if they didn't come? Anyway, he believes in men nonetheless. And you know it's funny; he says men don't believe in us fairies.'

'Ha!' The two laughed loudly at the irony, and the thought stayed with them, cheering them. Soon they reached Ferny Arch. Beside it were many clusters of reeds, ferns in shallow ditches, sparse stalks of hardy grasses, and flowers unknown anywhere else in the lea. Soggybog really was a wide place, easily

---

[13]     Great feather-bills are large birds, e.g. cranes, herons, geese, crows, etc.

big enough for all the fairies together. Bor'Tem built her home in one of the rare dry ditches. It was quiet, dark, and hidden, like Bur-duun's old home in Thistle Town. Then a wave of loneliness came over her so that she could not be consoled and the flowers blooming brightly did not cheer her, nor did the hopping greens whose spawn wobbled close by, not even Golden Orb itself could lift her melancholy state, so she shut herself inside, away from the world, and cried herself to sleep.

Golden Orb set, and the night was mild. Arthos and Tem, knowing nothing of Bor'Tem's loneliness, were still enjoying the novelty of Soggybog. Marsh creatures stirred and sang, making new noises for them to learn. Sprightly danced at the Bulrush theatre, and all besides Bor'Tem were happy and at peace. True, Arthos and Tem would miss Bur-duun greatly, but as yet they knew not how long she would be away, so why worry needlessly? And still, deep within them, they felt the strength of Barzad's love—though now, it seemed, it came at a price. Perhaps it was hasty to leave Thistle Town so suddenly, but while they enjoyed the welcome of Soggybog, this was far from their minds.

Their departure was not so far from Barzad's mind, however, and as they slept the reedy marsh slumber he paced the mossy floor of Thorny Tunnel, thinking of his own hasty mistake. He was so determined to send Bur-duun off with Scuri'Boo that it had never entered his head she might need time to tell her parents, and now they were all gone. Would others follow? He ranted in a voice that carried through the thistle heights. He wrung his hands, and all the while the fairies listened close by and worried in their beds.

'Wish I gave her time. Why did I send her off so soon?'
'Who is he talking about?' Horaf whispered to Shubar.
'Who is he talking *to*?' Shubar answered.
Grass Venture woke, disturbed by the confusion.

For a moment, Barzad thought quietly. *The whitetails—they would have waited another day.* And again he spoke aloud. 'Should have made them wait.'

Grass Venture protested at the noise.

'Shhh! It's okay. Go to sleep,' Shubar reassured him.

'Is it about the new thistle girl?' Horaf asked.

'Maybe she's not a thistle after all,' Shubar suggested. Still Barzad raved, but his voice became incoherent. They slept the night's remainder fitfully, wondering what the morning would bring. When at last it was discovered that Bur-duun had disappeared and that Bor'Tem and her parents had gone to the marsh, Thistle Town buzzed with talk, but none knew the reason. When further rumours told of her in Whitetail city with the lone fairy Scuri'Boo, they were no closer to understanding.

'Kuz'Aar works for Barzad. He would know,' the rising murmurs claimed, but where was he? After leaving Bur-duun and Scuri'Boo, he spent the following nights wandering under the sparkling fires, like a lone. Shubar eventually found him on the outskirts of the lea, where the fence is almost covered by tall grasses. He was sitting alone, head in his hands, eyes downward, staring at his feet. A lifetime of days passed for Kuz'Aar as he turned the situation over in his mind. Should he stay and wait for Bur-duun to return while his anger for Barzad grew ever stronger, or should he leave for Inner Lea and tell the fairies where she would find him? It was hard to imagine Bur-duun ever returning to Thistle Town. Perhaps she would go straight to Inner Lea herself. He eventually chose to go. He knew he would miss his thistle friends, but Ben'Tork, everyone's favourite, was already gone. How many others would follow? It was at this moment, as he sat thinking, that Shubar found him.

'Kuz'Aar! So this is where you've been.'

Kuz'Aar raised his eyes from their gloom and faced her. 'I'm leaving Thistle Town.'

'Why? What's the matter? You look awful.'

'When Bur-duun returns, will you tell her I'm with Ben'Tork in Dandelion Village?'

'But why? Don't you like it here anymore?'

'You just give her the message. Now I will go and tell Barzad.' And before the changing of the orbs, he stomped through Barzad's door. He had his rant ready, and Barzad listened.

'I never asked anything of you. I followed, like the other fairies, because you were brave. But you're not brave, Chief Barzad, who gets everyone else to go fetch. Oh, Kuz'Aar! Go away to the bog and find Bor'Tem! You remember Bor'Tem? Probably not. Well . . .'

'Now, hold on,' Barzad interrupted. 'What's all this about?'

Kuz'Aar had no idea he would hit such a sensitive nerve. He knew nothing of Bor'Tem's leaving, but seeing his aim was accurate, he continued.

'Always you've wanted to keep us apart, always keeping me away from the fun. Why should I work for you? And why should Scuri'Boo work for you either? He's not even a thistle.'

'Will you stop asking questions? Anyway, it's personal.'

'Of course it's personal! It's always been personal with you. You couldn't get near her because of me, so you sent me out to work and sent her away. Well, I'm off to Dandelion Village. You can find another fairy to enslave.' And with that he turned for Inner Lea as the first light of Golden Orb stretched across the expanse of yellow.

In that frightening moment, Barzad saw at last the error he had made. Scuri'Boo was no more a friend of Bur-duun than he was of any other fairy; it was Kuz'Aar she loved the most, and now he had separated them for he knew not how long. He thought of how they must feel and what he should do. If he called her back, the other fairies would see he had made an error and doubt him. If he left her there, she and Kuz'Aar would despise him. Already Arthos and Tem had left for Soggybog. He had made an enemy of Kuz'Aar, who had gone into the calming north of Inner Lea. How many others would follow? And what would become of Thistle Town? For Barzad, the fear of uncertainty was a desperate thing, but the fear of other fairies' uncertainty in him was far worse.

The only saving grace was the knowledge that Bur-duun and Kuz'Aar kept their relationship secret, so no other fairy would know of his mistake; only that he had sent Bur-duun away and then changed his mind and called her back. And call her back he must! How dearly he would have loved to avoid the awkwardness of admitting his mistake to her in front of Scuri'Boo. But for all his mistakes and arrogance, Barzad loved Bur-duun unconditionally and felt the flush of shame at his treatment of them both, so he forced himself onto his feet and made for the whitetail city without telling a soul.

# LOVERS APART

Bor'Tem felt refreshed after having her secret cry, and now the morning seemed bright and hopeful. Arthos and Tem, still determined not to worry, were cheerful and energetic. Sprightly-go-lightly would soon be here, eager to entertain the guests. Knowing that, Wui-bur invited Stooping Reed under the pretence that he and Bor'Tem could work on buttercup worship. Secretly, buttercup worship was far from his mind; he saw how it was between young Stooping Reed and Sprightly-go-lightly, and if it would only happen the union would have his hearty blessing. But Bor'Tem skipped off to Vi'Shay's favourite pond to talk of council business and watch the spawn of hopping greens wriggle their tails and swim for the first time, so they were left standing. Stooping Reed was suddenly aware of their real reason for being there, so when she came he was embarrassed and awkward in his shyness. Worse, she saw that he was embarrassed and understood why.

Soon it was midmorning. Kuz'Aar felt the heat of Golden Orb above him as he walked the long distance, alone, without a seed, heaving the heavy sighs of tough exertion. He just wanted to play—to be a fairy. Soon he would be in Dandelion Village, where everyone was at ease. He thought of Ben'Tork, who would be there.

'Lovely Ben'Tork, meek and kind. How does he love Barzad so much?'

They were as opposite as could be and yet the greatest of friends. He thought also of Bur-duun, who was now far away.

A wave of loneliness came over him, but he concentrated on Dandelion Village, which soon appeared over the crest of a small hill. It was lemon yellow with the bloom of many dandelions, drenched in the light of Golden Orb. Some were not fully opened, but others were nearly finished. These, Kuz'Aar noticed, were beginning to seed in the way thistles do. By now all the other fairies would know. He had missed out on a great event while he wandered around the barriers, thinking unhappy thoughts of Barzad. From as far away as Soggybog, even back to Thistle Town, the news would have swept. Dandelion seeds were like thistles! Perhaps there had been a party. This time anger did not consume him. 'I am here, and a seed is here. I will ride into Dandelion Village, and the breeze will be in my face.'

Laughing, he took a seed and clung to it. As the wind blew, he soared upwards to a great hilarious, height and was taken north, towards the towering branches of Gloomy Forest. Far below, he saw the beautiful, sleepy village where many dandelions bloomed in clusters. He lowered himself gently onto the ground, but there seemed to be no one about.

'Must be still dozing,' he thought aloud. 'This is the place for a lazy fairy like me.'

The seed, released from his grasp, soared again upwards. Kuz'Aar lay back and gazed as it floated away, changing direction. When the wind dipped, it remained suspended, and when the wind picked up again, it was gone. Kuz'Aar's eyes became droopy, as though the lovely seed cast a spell on him with some hidden magic, and soon he fell into a deep sleep.

Nearby, camouflaged against the flowering daisies, a young fairy looked on secretly. When she saw that Kuz'Aar was asleep, she came from her hiding place and crept up towards him. It was Peeping Bud. She put her face right up against his to see if she would recognise him, but she couldn't, so she ran off to tell somebody. When she returned with Tuss-kazuu, the stranger was already surrounded. Chief Tu'Hob, the Kazma-zan, was there with Ben'Tork. She loved Tu'Hob. She hardly knew

Ben'Tork. Also there were Gor'Teeb the fabulous, who played with her often, and High Wind, who held a seed.

'I was riding nearby and saw him,' High Wind said gently.

'Who is it?' inquired Daisy Petal not so gently as her friend. Excitement was obvious in her tone.

'That is Kuz'Aar of Thistle Town,' Ben'Tork answered. 'I know him well, but I wonder what brings him here.'

'Perhaps he has a message from Thorny Tunnel. I wonder is it urgent,' Tu'Hob suggested.

Kuz'Aar was no lover of urgency, and Ben'Tork knew a message from Thorny Tunnel might come too late if left to Kuz'Aar, so he nudged the sleeping Kuz'Aar to gently wake him. He slowly came to, yawned, stretched, and allowed his eyes to meet each face.

'Welcome to Inner Lea.' Tu'Hob stretched a hand in greeting, which Kuz'Aar took.

'Did Barzad send you? How is he?' This came from Ben'Tork, who was not always so direct.

'Barzad is Barzad.' This was followed by a pause, after which Kuz'Aar asked, 'Is there room for one more in Dandelion Village?'

An almost inaudible gasp of awareness came from the fairies as they understood in unison. Kuz'Aar had left Barzad for good.

'There is always room here for son of Aar.' Tu'Hob, smiling, led him gently towards a fragrant patch of wildflowers, where lunch was being served. They welcomed him in the quiet fashion of dandelions, calmly and without pomp and circumstance. Those who knew Kuz'Aar looked forward to his wit, but they soon saw a changed fairy and wondered what mischief lay behind his leaving Thistle Town so suddenly. There was sadness in him, and often he would stand alone facing the fence at the foot of Windy Hill. He seemed a paradox, at once glad to leave Barzad's authority but also missing his friends and the excitement of Thistle Town. He thought constantly of

Bur-duun, as she did of him in the deep underground dark while all the relentless digging and planning took place around her.

It was hard for Bur-duun not to feel divorced from the madness when her little heart was aching for the company of Kuz'Aar and the other fairies. In Scuri'Boo, loneliness was also taking its toll. His fairy eyes were not accustomed to the dark, and it was difficult to see what, if any, progress the whitetails were making. Frustration and impatience were obvious in his tone.

'This is horrible!' he sighed at last.

'I'm sick of it too.' Bur-duun glanced around in case a whitetail were nearby and added in a whisper, 'How do they live like this, underground in this . . . *mustiness?*'

'I can't see a thing.'

'I don't see Barzad here helping out. Why did he have to send us?'

'Well, I know why I'm here. It was Bor'Tem's and my idea that they should dig new runs here. But why you?' As soon as Scuri'Boo said it, he regretted mentioning Bor'Tem's name. He averted his eyes as Bur-duun bent her head and wiped away a single tear that made its way down her face to her wobbling chin.

'I miss Bor'Tem,' she said at last.

'I know you do.' He put his skinny little arm around her neck for comfort, but instead, a fresh wave of loneliness swept over her as she thought of Kuz'Aar's warm hold.

'Try to be positive.' Scuri'Boo wiped her wet face and kissed her shivering hands; he was unusually affectionate for a lone.

'Just think of the party they'll throw on our return. Every fairy in the lea will be there.'

At this Bur-duun laughed softly through her tears and said aloud a few names they both knew.

'Grass Venture.'

'Yes. Young Grass Venture will be there.'

'Horaf and Shubar.'

'Yes.'

'Kuz'Aar.'

'Him too.'

'Especially him!'

A pause followed while Scuri'Boo wondered why she should include Kuz'Aar so emphatically. Slowly it dawned on him why he and Bur-duun had been thrown together and sent to the deep, dark city beyond the lea.

'Oh. I see . . . I think I understand why we're here.'

'You do?'

'Perhaps Barzad believes it is me you love.'

'Aw! What! Why?' Bur-duun was laughing properly now.

'Well, he was very angry with me recently, unnecessarily so, even for Barzad, and his thoughts of you are obvious.'

She blushed slightly at this reminder of his constant attention.

'You have never told him about Kuz'Aar, have you? Your reasons are your own. Could you have let him believe it was someone else, like me?'

Bur-duun remembered with shame the lie she told, pretending she had to meet Scuri'Boo just so she could spend time with Kuz'Aar. As she did this, Young Buck and Little Doe came laughing down the run. They stopped suddenly when they saw the two fairies. Bur-duun quickly wiped away the remainder of her tears, but it was too late, the whitetails saw. Young Buck looked at Little Doe, unsure what to say, but Little Doe was better equipped.

'Are you feeling unwell?'

'Oh yes. That's it. Just a little unwell.' Bur-duun grabbed at the excuse offered.

'We thought we'd introduce some of our friends,' Young Buck said. 'Maybe it's not such a good time.' He turned to go.

'Oh, stay! Please.'

'Really? If you're sure?'

By now the other whitetails were cramming into the run, craning their necks to see the two fairies. Most had never seen a fairy before. They were excited from the digging, and there was steam and heat from their fur.

'This is Stony Burrow,' Little Doe began.

'Hello.'

'Nice to meet you.' Stony Burrow moved aside so another could take his place.

'And Violet Paw.'

'Hello.'

'Rushing River.'

More names were mentioned, but the fairies could not see the faces farther back. These were Scent of Spring, Leafy Nibble, and Bounding Haunches. When all the whitetails were introduced, everyone went outside to the last of the midsummer evening. The grass was short, so it was easy for the fairies to move around and see. Daisies were abundant; Bur-duun rested herself on a leaf while a whitetail—Violet Paw, she thought—nibbled nearby. Scuri'Boo stretched his legs and cart-wheeled, glad to be out in the scented air.

'Fabulous work we're doing, eh?'

Bur-duun looked round to find the voice behind her. It was Chief Big Buck. She had never seen him properly before. He was enormous and brown, and a sweet scent came from his fur.

'If you think so. I can't tell.'

'Oh! It's good work, all right. You'll see it soon; don't worry.'

'Not soon enough!'

Big Buck raised his head and looked southwest to Thistle Town. 'You miss your friends. Little Doe told me.'

Bur-duun picked at a seed that landed some time ago and was preparing to germinate in the summer heat. 'Little Doe is perceptive.'

'You don't want to be here. Why are you?'

'I was sent!' Bur-duun tried to stop herself from crying all over again, but the directness of Big Bucks approach threw her, and she could not contain herself. This time her tears were furious, and there was no wiping away the hot river that flowed. Her breath was quick, and soon she was a shuddering mess, surrounded by concerned whitetails.

'Oh now, what's this?' came from one of the does.

'Who sent you when you did not want to come?' This was from Big Buck.

'It was all a misunderstanding.' It was coming out of Bur-duun's mouth before she knew the answer herself.

'He thought I was in love with Scuri'Boo. We let him think I was, but I just wanted to stay with Kuz'Aar. Oh, what have I done?'

The whitetails gathered closer round her while she tidied herself up again. Scuri'Boo, nearby, listened intently as she explained it all.

'Barzad wouldn't leave me alone. I didn't tell him about Kuz'Aar. I was afraid of what he would do, so we pretended I wanted to go and see Scuri'Boo. We didn't think he'd let me go; we didn't even think he'd believe us.'

Scuri'Boo sat quietly, eating. A small whitetail was talking to him, describing how he noticed his fur was healthier since the fairies arrived. Scuri'Boo was only listening with one ear; the other was concentrating on Bur-duun. He was a little offended at being used as an excuse, but his heart went out to Bur-duun, whose fear of Barzad was obvious.

'Barzad. I've heard of him once before, and I didn't much like him then.' Chief Big Buck recalled the meeting he had with Scuri'Boo when the whitetails first wanted to rebuild and Barzad refused to help. Big Buck looked up and found in the distance the glow of Golden Orb, falling fast. The clouds, in crimson silk arrayed, lost their grip, and she sunk lower as they faded into grey. It was time for the whitetails to go underground, so he gave the word, and they followed in simple obedience. The fairies too, made their way down, slowly, silently lagging.

# A BAD DAY FOR BARZAD

The last light faded, and Barzad worried his way through the night, afraid of dark creatures that hid. But he would crawl through any fear to see Bur-duun at the other side, though she would stand silent and unsmiling. From the beginning she despised him, and he knew not of any way he could warm her to him, but how was he to know what only a sister could see? For while Bor'Tem threw him her soul so eagerly and he ignored her, oblivious and bored, Bur-duun could see how it crushed her heart.

In that long night as Barzad walked, nature was all around him. Dew fell on June grass, and the humid soil smelled of earth. All the world would be right if he could just get to her and explain. He wished he had a seed—or a spell. He wished he had Kuz'Aar's charm. Now that would be worth something! It occurred to Barzad that he had underestimated Kuz'Aar. He laughed bitterly at the irony, for a lazy fairy, Kuz'Aar had been busy, very busy, right under his nose.

*Well, good luck to Kuz'Aar,* he thought. *Kuz'Aar, the lazy fairy, who can humiliate the chief of all thistles, berate me, and then take the north walk, where Ben'Tork will greet him. He will win dandelion hearts and turn my Ben'Tork against me.*

Unsure of the way, he struggled in the dark. If only the sparkling fires were not shrouded in thick cloud, he would not be so lost, and his footing was treacherous. Unknowing and inadvertently, Barzad disturbed a poppy. It was not injured; instead, it woke from sleep and looked as Barzad passed, and as it did, many seeds fell onto the parched soil. After that night it propagated abundantly, and years later there were many, all because the fairy, Barzad, touched it, took its loneliness and stored it with his own.

As morning peeped over the crest of Windy Hill, the hedgerow was noisy with birdsong. Feather-bills flittered in and out, flapping their wings, alarming Barzad at every few steps. All night long he found not a single seed, so he had to travel the old-fashioned way. He was exhausted.

*How long before I find Bur-duun?* he thought. *How long before I get another piece of food? And how will I find these beasts when their great city is underground?* Barzad saw he had also underestimated Scuri'Boo, who knew the whitetails, knew their ways, and could easily find where they lived. He knew he must get across the hedgerow to the other side, but he would not go through it for fear of disturbing feather-bills. It was not until Golden Orb was high in her midday seat that Barzad came upon the answer to his conundrum in the form of a gate. He had no idea it was a gate; to him it was just another man-made barrier, but this one was not unlike the fence at Soggybog, so big a fairy could easily walk right under it as though it weren't there at all. This he did, and at last, beyond the barriers, in the far place, Barzad could look around.

The great four-legs grazed here too, but today they were blocked off by another man-made barrier, far down the hawthorn line of hedgerow. Where he stood, the grass was nibbled short by whitetails. He could walk right up towards the hill, when his energy would let him—but first he must get food and a place to rest, and his chances of finding either were slim in this wide space, no place for a fairy. Barzad felt exposed, despite the fresh daisy smell and the peaceful air, for large feather-bills cawed and pecked the ground beside him.

'No place here for food,' he mumbled to himself, starting to feel weak from hunger. He turned back and found a jagged rock jutting out from the baked soil. He lay down by its warmth while the world forgot him.

When Golden Orb moved so that Barzad's rock was in the shade, he woke drenched with rain, thirsty, and starving. He struggled to his feet and wobbled onwards. Whether he was going in the right direction he didn't know; in his exhaustion, he paid little attention. But soon he found evidence of whitetails along the hedgerow, and followed onwards until he came upon a dark, earthy hole leading downwards through the floor of the world. As the rain stopped, the whitetails began to emerge in ones and twos. Barzad surveyed them and, after judging who he assumed to be the leader, approached confidently.

'I am Barzad of Thistle Town. Please bring to me the two fairies whom I sent to you.'

Stony Burrow and Violet Paw looked at each other, puzzled, and began to talk in coded whispers that Barzad could not understand. All they had ever heard of Barzad was negative, and now they worried for Scuri'Boo and Bur-duun. Stony Burrow turned to him.

'You wait here.' This said, he hopped towards another hole in the earth, where Bounding Haunches and Scent of Spring were just coming out.

Barzad watched as they talked, their faces looking serious, and darted quick glances in his direction. He was beginning to feel unsure and thought to himself, *What if the whitetails don't want to return them? Everyone will be lonely for them. The whitetails will war with us. The whole lea will rise up against me.*

At last one whitetail came towards him. It was Bounding Haunches; his movement was slow, deliberate, and defiant. Barzad stood to him, chin out in expectation.

'No fairies here. Fairies left long time ago.'

'Left?'

'Left. Gone. No fairies here.' Bounding Haunches turned to go, anxious to hide the lie.

'Wait! When did they go?'

'Long time ago,' he answered, not looking at Barzad directly. Scent of Spring came to his aid.

'Look. You see our new town here is nearly finished. We're very grateful to you for sending them, but they weren't needed for long, so we sent them home.'

'But . . .' Barzad's voice broke. 'They never came home.'

'Maybe they go to bog place where other fairies live . . .'

Obviously Scuri'Boo had been telling the whitetails what a great place Soggybog was. Barzad did not want other creatures to know the fairies were segregated, and the mention of Soggybog evoked in him an instant feeling of anger, which he should have kept to himself.

'No! I tell you!' he shouted, stamping his tiny, petulant foot. 'They would have come to me first.'

This provoked the wrong reaction in the whitetails, who shrugged carelessly at his bad manners and hopped away without a backward glance. Stony Burrow and Violet Paw disappeared down into the earth to find the fairies and prevent them coming out where Barzad would find them.

Barzad, left alone to contemplate his error, stood looking at his toes in shame and berated himself. 'No welcome here for a stupid fairy.' Weak from hunger and exhaustion, soaked through with rain, and colder than he had ever been before, he turned and found again the dark, twittering hedgerow that led home. Feather-bills were out again, laughing loudly, as if to spite the recent rain, but Barzad didn't notice, his fear of them forgotten in his new panic. What had become of them? Had they gotten lost? What was he to tell the other fairies? What will they do to him?

'I'll never be trusted again,' he said aloud. 'And all my friends will leave me. Thistle Town will be deserted. There I will wait alone, but Bur-duun might never return.'

Under the hedgerow he let himself drop to the shaded soil. The loose bark was unpalatable, too hard and dry. He gnawed at it in vain until eventually he succumbed to exhaustion and slept where he lay. But as he slept in semi-consciousness, a conversation occurred between the weeds nearby.

'Hey folks! Look at this!'

'What is it, Scutch?'

'I think it's a fairy.'

'Oh! How lovely. I've never seen a fairy before.' This came from Groundsel, who bent forward slightly to see.

'I think there's something wrong with it,' Scutch thought aloud.

'Maybe it's just tired,' Chickweed said.

'Or maybe it's just hungry,' said Dock.

'Well, what do fairies eat?' Groundsel was the most practical.

'They eat . . . us.'

'Don't be ridiculous, Chickweed.'

'Chickweed is right,' Dock said darkly, and in the silence that ensued, he carefully placed a leaf of his own against the blackberry briar and ripped a small chunk from himself.

Chickweed tried to do the same, but he couldn't reach. Their bravery was acknowledged, and solemnly, silently, the others joined in the ritual until a small pile of leaves and petals was gathered and directed through the gentle wind to Barzad's feet.

In the shady paths of Thorny Tunnel, the needy soil was waiting for Barzad. But he left in a hurry to seek the special fairies he had sent away in error, and would not soon return. There would be many questions, and he had no explanation to give but that he had made a grave mistake. Still exhausted, starving and cold, he lay beneath the hedgerow. The weeds looked on, concerned for his welfare. In the cool, rising breeze, Barzad shivered and woke, slowly remembering the horror of his day. He rubbed his eyes and focused on the pile of petals at his feet. He looked about him, but nobody was around. Somebody had put them there, and he knew that he was not forgotten, even in this dark place.

'Golden Orb has helped me in my time of need.' He spoke aloud, looking at the evening sky, and he noticed nothing strange about the weeds, though they nudged each other gently and laughed lightly in the whispering wind and rustling hawthorn hedgerow. But long after Barzad fortified himself and left, still the weeds remembered, and they told their seeds, and their seeds' seeds, of the time an ailing fairy lay among them until they made him well.

Barzad stood on a steep stretch of Windy Hill, where the four-legs had recently grazed. They were penned into another part of the pasture now, but their scent was still on the grass, sweet and overpowering in the evening air. At this height he could see the whole lea. Straight across and farthest away, the marsh lay wild and untidy. At this distance nothing was clear but the tall, rigid reeds. Barzad had never been interested in Soggybog, but now it looked untamed and fascinating. Nearer and greener was Inner Lea, where Ben'Tork was some miniscule dot, hidden by yellow and white dandelions gone to seed. There were many dandelions, so many seeds to enjoy. Truly, Inner Lea was just as blessed as Thistle Town. Barzad saw that he had again underestimated someone; this time it was Tu'Hob and his great, peaceful village where the customs of the past still remained. To the left lay his favourite place. Even from here, Thistle Town was full of life. Large weeds stood proud and fantastic, blooming in the summer heat, and he could just make out the pink heads of foxgloves bobbing in conversation. Turning, he saw in the distance the upright figure of some creature moving among the great-four-legs. What creature could it be? So far away, it seemed but a shadow, and Barzad did not realise it was a man.

Here in the pasture, dandelions also bloomed. None close to him were in seed, but Barzad knew it would not be long before he found one, and then he could ride over the field and find the missing fairies. Nearby a small group of speckled feather-bills[14] pecked the ground for worms, but Barzad was not afraid. He had greater worries, and the feather-bills might even be able to help. Slowly, he stepped up to them and made his presence known.

'I am the fairy Barzad.'

The nearest feather-bill moved away. Taken aback, but undaunted, Barzad stepped up to another.

'I am the fairy Barzad. Have you seen my friends?'

This one also moved away, but instead of calmly settling back, the whole flock flew in unison upwards in looping acrobatics, using all the sky, until they finally moved northwards to Gloomy Forest, where they landed silently in the tree shadows for the night. Barzad despaired; he would have to spend another night alone in the wide, exposed pasture, where any creature of night might come upon him. He would find no fairies in this dark; he would have to continue his search in the morning. And so, finding a small hollow in the land, he curled up, covered his tiny body with blades of grass, and lay in shivering wakefulness under the round White Orb and silvery sheets of cloud.

Shaded by the briars and neglected thicket, away from the summer heat, Uulor was at home, and he was not alone. Boo had come over to moan about Barzad, for whom she had lost a great deal of respect. When she had not seen Scuri'Boo for days, though she normally heard from him often, she went looking throughout the lea and it was Shubar who told her where he had gone. Since Kuz'Aar left for the dandelions, Thistle Town was alive with talk, and it became known that Bur-duun and Scuri'Boo were sent to the whitetail city. Without even a moment's notice, Scuri'Boo was off beyond the barriers for nobody knew how long, and Boo missed him terribly. It was all Barzad's fault.

---

[14]    Speckled feather-bills are starlings.

'Why should he be doing Barzad's bidding, anyway? Since when is Barzad his chief?'

'Hush now. You won't get anywhere by thinking like that,' Uulor tried to soothe her.

'I've a good mind to go round to Thistle Town!'

'And do what?'

'Give that Barzad a piece of my mind, that's what!'

'Now, that's not a good idea, is it?'

'Whyever not?'

'Barzad may have reasons we don't know about.'

'Like what?'

'When has Scuri ever done something he had no mind to do? For all we know, this may have been his idea. You know how much he liked to talk to those whitetails.'

For a while Boo said nothing as she thought over his words and drank slowly from a nutshell of water. At last she asked him, 'What are we to do?

'We are to wait, I suppose.'

'I'm lonely for him.'

'So am I.' Uulor took Boo gently from her seat and held her to him until she was soothed. Affection had never been his strongpoint, but now it came naturally with kind words; and reassurance from Uulor was always welcome because he knew many things other fairies would not. So Boo stayed with Uulor in his dark little house, and he was gentle to her, cheering her spirits until she forgot her anger with Barzad. They recalled the old place, before the long journey, when they were young and Barzad was just a boy. Many lovely things had kept them there, even as they feared the winds of change Uulor warned them of. They resolved not to move until they had to. Then the men came and if the fairies could see now the false lake and reservoir, they would not recognise the place at all, but perhaps they would not have disliked it either.

# Kuz'Aar

Kuz'Aar was not used to the long lie-ins of Dandelion Village, and he became fidgety and frustrated. Eventually he gave up and found a tiny puddle in which to wash. Quietly, he began to hum to himself a song Bur-duun taught him, but it made him lonely for her, so he stopped. She was away in the whitetail city, the far place only Scuri'Boo knew, and she would not likely return soon, so he did as he always did when his hurt was too great, he filed it away in some recess of his mind so that it could not be recalled easily. He continued to bathe in silence, but there was no fun in it, and his morning was spent sitting bored and alone, waiting for some action. At last, High Wind came skipping round a flowery bend and stopped abruptly.

'You're Kuz'Aar, aren't you?'

'Yes.'

'This is bright and early. You're not so lazy as they say.'

'No, I don't suppose I am.' Kuz'Aar laughed at the young fairy's honesty and stepped up to him, that they might walk together.

'I am High Wind.'

'Yes, I remember. So! What are we doing?' Kuz'Aar was anxious for some excitement.

'Well . . . I thought I might ride the seed. Would you like to come too?'

'Will another seed be easy to find?' Kuz'Aar knew there were plenty in Dandelion Village now, but he thought best to ask out of politeness. Without a word, High Wind turned back the way he had come, directing the newcomer to a mound of dandelion heads.

'Take your pick!'

Kuz'Aar did. 'Then we're off!' And up they climbed in virtual steps as their seeds were taken ever higher into the blue summer sky. They rode for hours until Inner Lea grew chill with greying clouds. Rain came in big, heavy drops, so Kuz'Aar and High Wind had to land. Besides, it was time for food anyway. Gently they allowed their seeds to descend and watched as the downpour filled gaps and cracks of thirsty earth. Ben'Tork waved and ran to them, smiling and excited. 'How was your ride?'

'Oh, the wind is good today,' High Wind answered. 'Hope you enjoyed that, Kuz'Aar.'

Kuz'Aar had a fabulous time, if his wide grin was anything to go by. A group had gathered nearby where food was being served; a light nibble of fallen petals, grass tips, and dew collected earlier that morning. As they seated themselves comfortably on the hardened earth and ate quietly, Kuz'Aar thought to himself that he might easily come to love young High Wind, who had made a lasting impression on him and helped keep his mind free from dark thoughts of Barzad. Gor-Teeb wandered over, humming sweetly, and sat herself down amongst them.

Evening descended slowly as they sang and danced together. Kuz'Aar and High Wind lazed on the soft grass, dipping their feet into a puddle made by the recent rain. Gor'Teeb, nearby, sung softly to herself as she watched two figures approaching from the direction of Thistle Town on dandelion seeds. Even at a distance she could hear the high-pitched screech of female laughter and said aloud, 'Who could that be?'

The others stood up to see what thistle, indeed, could laugh so heartily, when Kuz'Aar spoke only of gloom in Thistle Town. Grass Venture was soon recognised by his curly locks of reddish gold, and at his side was the new thistle girl, Floating

Bliss. He had come to take her away from there, away from the speculation and the whispers that made everyone so unhappy. The pair landed gently and came down from their dandelion seeds.

'Good day, Grass Venture.' Ben'Tork was looking at Floating Bliss. 'And might we guess who this lovely girl is?'

'This is Floating Bliss, our newest arrival!'

'Hello, everybody.' Floating Bliss's voice was soft and velvety. She looked to Grass Venture shyly but happily.

'My name is Ben'Tork. I'm a great friend of your chief, Barzad.' Instantly, Ben'Tork wished he hadn't mentioned Barzad, but he carried on as if he had not blundered. 'And this is Kuz'Aar, also a friend of . . .'

Kuz'Aar curled his lips and glared at him.

'Yes . . . Well . . . and this is Gor'Teeb, the fabulous!'

'Hello.'

'And High Wind. Now you know everybody.' Ben'Tork allowed himself time to recover before talking again, and as he was silent, Gor'Teeb filled the gap.

'So you are the new thistle girl. You're really quite famous, you know? The whole lea is talking about you.'

'Really?'

'Oh yes! You just wandered into Thistle Town as if you knew where you were going,' Gor'Teeb said. 'That's quite amazing. You did very well not to get lost.'

'Well, I did know where I was going. At least, I sort of knew.'

'And where did you come from originally?' Kuz'Aar asked.

'I'm not sure. There was long grass, but it was night, and I think I changed direction often before light.' Kuz'Aar sat up, interested. He asked her many more questions and let her answer slowly. She talked a long time, not intimidated by his interest. Something about him made her feel relaxed and less shy. Into the night she talked about herself, describing her journey to Thistle Town, the long grass, the weeds, how she felt her wings flutter but couldn't use them, the scents she smelled, the flowers she saw. Kuz'Aar thought he could retrace her footsteps, given a chance, and as she talked, High Wind listened to her voice and said nothing—nor would he get the chance, for Uulor was on his way to retrieve her.

In the new burrows, whitetails and fairies whispered in worried tones.

'Did Barzad say what he wanted us for?' Scuri'Boo asked.

'No. We pretended you were gone.'

Some whitetails looked round uneasily, as though the thistle chief were a real threat. All they knew of Barzad were the bad things they heard, and they had the impression of an evil despot who made the fairies unhappy. They knew none of the good things, his hearty love for all fairies, his great energy and sense of fun, or his being first to ride the seed, bravely risking what no fairy had ever done before. Scuri'Boo could see that he and Bur-duun had led them to this belief and sought to rectify his error.

'He's really not all bad, you know.'

The whitetails scoffed.

'Well, I don't much want to meet him again,' said Stony Burrow.

'No! He does have some redeeming qualities,' Bur-duun began, but then she couldn't think of any and became quiet again. In her silent state she secretly thought it would have been nice to see Barzad again, grumpy and arrogant though he was. It was a long time since she had seen another fairy besides Scuri'Boo, and Barzad might have told her some news of her friends and family. A wave of regret flushed through Bur-duun, who felt herself constantly drawn back to Thistle Town as though some wondrous joy awaited her there.

Scuri'Boo was also homesick. The whitetails saw that they might have made a mistake. A few whitetails shuffled aside to let Big Buck enter.

'Everybody okay?'

'Yes, we're all okay. Little Doe was a big shaken, but she's fine now.' This came from Young Buck.

Now that Big Buck was there to take control, the whitetails began to leave so the fairies could talk alone with him.

'You sure you're okay?'

'Yes. Yes. We're fine . . . Really, he is a good fairy.'

'Hmmm.' Big Buck was not convinced. 'Well, anyway, I suppose your work here is done. We still have a lot of digging to do, obviously, but maybe we could postpone some of it, and Scuri'Boo, perhaps you could come back by yourself and help us a little later in the year.'

'You think so? Really?' Bur-duun could not hide her excitement and received a reproachful look from Scuri'Boo.

'Eh hem. That is to say . . . I mean . . . Barzad might need us.'

'It's okay. I understand.' Big Buck chuckled. 'Living underground is good for us whitetails but not so good for fairies.'

'Well, we thank you for your hospitality,' said Scuri'Boo.

'Oh yes! You've all been lovely to us.'

'We could finish this burrow here tonight, and then tomorrow, you fairies can leave for . . . for your Barzad.' Big Buck turned to go up the run to the open air, but he stopped halfway. 'Oh! And we will have a farewell get-together. I know how you fairies like to party.'

For a moment all was dark as his large body filled the mouth of the run, and then daylight returned. Bur-duun hopped from one leg to the other, waving her arms around in excitement.

'We're going home, we're going home. *We're going home!*' She grabbed Scuri'Boo by the arms and brought him dancing round a circle, laughing. At first he worried that they were letting the whitetails down, but her excitement was infectious, and he quickly became giddy. They skipped together out of the run into the shining rays of Golden Orb and saw Big Buck talking to a small group. Some looked in their direction as he spoke, which made the fairies feel wonderfully important. He was organising their farewell party. Truly, they were going home. Home to the rugged ground of Weedy Lea, where cracked, dry soil was shaded by long grass gone to seed, and where Kuz'Aar waited; home to all their friends, where parties were wild and nectar was plentiful; home to lonely Boo, who paced and moaned, waiting for her boy.

Bur-duun and Scuri'Boo feasted, surrounded by whitetails. The city was alive with excitement; gentle does mothered their young litters, bucks bounced and cuffed each other in mock fights. When White Orb rose for predatory night-bills, they hid underground and slept, but the two fairies stayed awake and sang until the morning dew began to glisten with light reflected. The whitetails rose. First to awaken were Young Buck and Little Doe, who would enjoy the pleasure of bringing the fairies home. Out in the open air, all good-byes were said. After a pause, the fairies climbed onto the backs of their bearers, and the four wordlessly moved west to Weedy Lea. There was no urgency with Young Buck and Little Doe. Frequently they stopped to nibble daisies in the short grass, but when they moved on, hopping gently, they made short work of the field.

The group arrived in Thistle Town while many fairies were still asleep, but Horaf and Shubar had washed already. The two whitetails veered towards the long grass for cover, as was their nature, and Bur-duun was soon reminded of where she and Kuz'Aar used to hide. In an instant, a wave of love swept over her. She was sure Kuz'Aar and her family would never have stayed with Barzad, but wherever they were in the lea, she would be with them all soon. Kuz'Aar and she would waste no more time hiding their affection, they would shout of their love from the rooftops of the world, and Barzad may learn to like it.

Horaf heard a nearby shuffle and looked up from his doodles in the soil. Instantly he recognised his two friends being borne like royalty by the whitetails and nudged Shubar, pointing in their direction. Everybody—weeds, whitetails, and others if they had the chance—were only too delighted to carry the fairies, for they were the chosen creatures and to carry them would be no burden but a gift. The fairies could not see this, but it was known in all nature that Golden Orb loved them the most, and there was never a grudge held against them, because they were most loved by nature too. Horaf and Shubar quickly woke up the neighbourhood, gathering a crowd to follow them. Bur-duun steered Little Doe back to Thorny Tunnel, assuming Barzad would be there, but when she climbed down and tapped on his door, there was no answer. Scuri'Boo questioned the faces gathered around them.

'Nobody knows where he is,' said a voice at the back.

'No. We haven't seen him in ages,' another said, and this was confirmed by many murmurs and nods.

'Well, how long has he been gone?' Bur-duun asked. 'Days?'

'Days and days,' said Horaf.

'Well, he was in Whitetail City only recently. The whitetails sent him away.'

Little Doe and Young Buck looked at each other, ashamed. Obviously Barzad was well loved and sadly missed. They had judged him wrongly. Uulor came to the crowd with Grass Venture and Floating Bliss on either side. Scuri'Boo ran to him, and his display of affection left little doubt about who his father was. Grass Venture quietly explained to Floating Bliss who Bur-duun and Scuri'Boo were and why they had been away.

Bur-duun was very taken by the new thistle girl. Was this the lovely surprise that pulled her back to the lea when she was in the whitetail city? In the absence of Barzad, Horaf began the party, and soon Thistle Town was filled with music and dance. While no one was looking, he snatched Grass Venture from the crowd and brought him to a quiet place.

'Where is the seed you came here on?'

'Am I in trouble? I was just showing Floating Bliss . . .'

'No, no. You're not in trouble.' Horaf was laughing through his urgency. 'But we need those seeds. You didn't let them go, did you?'

'No. I tied them down, like you showed me.' Grass Venture was in no hurry.

'Well, come on! We have to spread the word!'

'Oh. Okay.' Grass Venture ran to a nearby nettle and pulled the seeds out from a cluster of leaves. 'Where do you want me to go, Dandelion Village or Soggybog?'

'You do Soggybog. Make sure to tell Bor'Tem her sister is back,' said Horaf, and the two flew off in opposite directions to spread the good news. Grass Venture loved Bor'Tem well, and Horaf was glad to give him the joy of telling her Bur-duun had returned. Inwardly, he was glad to give the news to Dandelion Village. To Horaf and Shubar, Kuz'Aar's reasons for leaving Thistle Town were obvious in hindsight. He was always sneaking off with Bur-duun to giggle in the long grass. Kuz'Aar would return to greet her with Ben'Tork and his blade-whistle. Thistle Town would be like old times if only Barzad would return. During the gusty, short ride north, Hoarf became lonely for Barzad, his old friend who would not enjoy the party but sit alone in some far place while all the other fairies acted as if nothing were wrong.

Awaiting their return, Shubar kept the party going, but it was difficult. Without Barzad, the occasion had no flow, no charisma, and she missed him. Boo had come to berate Barzad, but finding him still gone and Scuri'Boo back, all notions of a confrontation were wiped away. She skipped to Uulor and clung to him as though it were he who orchestrated their return, but little did she know that as she did, he was privately devising a way to bring back Barzad. Uulor knew that Barzad meant no harm, destructive though he was, and if Barzad could suddenly disappear, perhaps there was something out there, beyond the lea, that the fairies should be wary of.

Exclamations of joy woke him from his thoughtfulness. The dandelions had arrived. Kuz'Aar barely had time to climb down from his seed before Bur-duun knocked him over and rained a shower of kisses on his face so that he turned puce with delight and embarrassment. Kuz'Aar also met again the lovely Floating Bliss, who had impressed him so hugely on her recent visit. High Wind, who had come along, was determined not to waste more time with wordless admiration, and strove to meet her lively chat with something equally entertaining.

Kuz'Aar became hyperactive, which was unusual and worth seeing. He grabbed Floating Bliss and High Wind each by an arm and danced around as though intoxicated with dandelion milk. When he settled down, Bur-duun was beside him, so he left the young ones alone.

# UULOR MEETS THE WHITETAILS

Uulor extricated himself from the party and slid away into the dark evening to find lonely Barzad. *Perhaps he went from Thistle Town to find Scuri'Boo and Bur-duun,* Uulor thought, but Barzad would never find them now beyond the lea, nor would he return empty handed. As if by magic, a stray dandelion seed floated by, and he grabbed it. Unsure how to ride, he rose anyway into the cloudless air and allowed himself to be taken southwards to the pasture where the new whitetail city was. It seemed almost pointless trying to find one single fairy in this dark, but still Uulor knew he must try. He had a vague idea where he was going and steered awkwardly in that direction, trying hard to keep his seed balanced. He could feel it getting easier as the night wore on, and when dawn approached, a dark and silent movement in the hedgerow told Uulor the whitetails were up. He steered towards them, shouting as he went, and in the first early light he could see a whitetail's ears shift upward, erect and listening to his tiny voice.

Stony Burrow tensed, prepared to stamp his foot, but quickly Uulor was beside him.

'I am the lone fairy Uulor,' he started. 'We thank you for returning our friends to us safely.' Stony Burrow relaxed and began to nibble the short grass.

'And your friends, Young Buck and Little Doe, they have returned too?'

'Yes, they are over there.' Stony Burrow looked up towards another corner of the field.

In the distance Uulor could see the two whitetails talking to another, much larger one, obviously their leader.

'I'm looking for our friend Barzad.'

'Yes, I suppose you are.' Stony Burrow moved down to Uulor. Uulor came closer and touched Stony Burrow on his furry paw. They connected in careful affection so that a bond of trust was made.

'We mistook Barzad for a bad fairy. We are truly sorry for our error...'

'Barzad is an arrogant fairy!' Uulor interrupted with more emphasis than he intended. Then he continued more softly, 'The error was his.'

'Thank you.' Stony Burrow was clearly relieved. 'I will take you to our chief.'

Uulor climbed up onto him, and they made towards Chief Big Buck. Stony Burrow alerted the other whitetails to their approach, so that upon reaching the far end of the field, they were surrounded by many.

Uulor introduced himself again, this time to the whole crowd, tiny in their midst but smiling and undaunted. He touched them each on a paw, humbling himself before them, and instantly they warmed to his mild nature. It would be a few hours yet before broad daylight, so Uulor had plenty of time to talk and listen to the whitetails. He asked many questions about their underground city, and they showed it to him. Secretly he was afraid to delve into the earth and when he found the total darkness, he liked it even less and felt for Scuri'Boo and Bur-duun and the time they spent down there. But the whitetails sensed his fear when he clutched more tightly to their fur and brought him back up into the day.

'Not a fan?' someone said, laughing.

'But it's not just a dark hole, you know,' said Violet Paw 'at least, not anymore. The fairies made it special.'

'Yes. Oh yes,' they all echoed.

'Magic fairies,' came from a small voice, whose owner Uulor couldn't see—obviously the most inquisitive of a new litter.

'Why magic?' asked Uulor.

'Magic. Yes. Oh! Wonderful.' They all began at once shouting over each other so that Uulor laughed heartily at their compliment.

'It is true.' This, from Big Buck, made them stop their blather instantly. Uulor listened, enthralled, as Big Bug explained about the whitetails' newfound vigour and how their pelts had improved since the fairies arrived. All the creatures and weeds could sense it, so how could the fairies not notice their own brilliance? A moment of silence followed when he was done. Uulor was moved beyond speaking. This was news indeed, and a lump came to his throat. The whitetails saw he was overcome, and some hopped away so that he could dry his eyes without embarrassment.

'We must help him find Barzad,' whispered Bounding Haunches to Little Doe when they were far enough away. Without further discussion each whitetail moved in a different direction, calling and searching for Barzad. And they had no fear of kestrels or other predators because Uulor was with them. Uulor was also fearless because he knew Golden Orb was watching from her low morning throne, and she cared for them all. Finally they found poor Barzad, lying wet in the dewy grass.

The Soggybog fairies had found seeds and made their way south. Grass Venture was wiped out with tiredness but glad to continue and reluctant to miss any more of the party.

'And how did she look? Was she in good form?' Bor'Tem was so excited. She knew she was bombarding him with questions, but she couldn't help it.

'What were the whitetails like? Were they nice to her?' Arthos was worse.

'Shhh, Arthos,' said Tem. 'Just concentrate on your riding.'

Back in Thistle Town, the party was in full swing. When a crowd of whitetails arrived with Uulor, Boo wondered how she had not missed him. A wide circle was made, to give Big Buck room, and Barzad came down from his heavy shoulders. Deep, grateful silence was followed by a thistle eruption. Barzad was back. The great, wonderful, charismatic Barzad, whom every thistle loved beyond understanding, had returned. A wave of relief flowed through the long grass of Thistle Town. Deep into the lea it carried through the wind, until the lea was awake with joy. Those that were left behind in Dandelion Village and in Soggybog, the lones, and everyone else understood in one magic moment, all was well. The fairies had made it through a crisis. Even Arthos and Tem were relieved, regardless of how he had treated their daughters, for Bur-duun was back. All was forgiven.

Uulor saw that, in finding Barzad, he had saved them from more needless worry. With this knowledge, energy surged through him. Worry was what made the fairies downtrodden. Worry failed them. Once the worry of Barzad was lifted, Uulor saw how the fairies reacted, they laughed where before there was fear, their wings fluttered where before there was limpness. The words sung in Uulor's head, but he kept them down. 'Magic fairies.' Was the young whitetail right?

With uproarious laughter, the Soggybog fairies arrived on seeds they were clearly not used to riding. All of Weedy Lea was united in celebration. Barzad saw Bur-duun and sprinted to his musty hut in search of some stem-juice to give as a peace offering, but Kuz'Aar had beaten him to it. No matter; Hazy Mellow was already working on new juice, fresh from the foxtail lilies. Shubar was off hosting duty now that Barzad was back, so she went to Horaf. Together they danced and played like children, but away from the crowd in the days to follow, they saw how Barzad was with Floating Bliss, and they worried. He would not leave her near High Wind, the dandelion boy, and favoured Grass Venture instead. Barzad saw before the dandelion himself that she had let High Wind into her heart, and sought to rectify this by tormenting Grass Venture, who was no more interested in Floating Bliss than he was in any other friend.

In Barzad there was chaos and confusion, which made him feel as if his world were tumbling down just as he found it again. He wanted Floating Bliss for Thistle Town and himself because she was so lovely, but she was having none of it. And it looked as if she were well able to stand up to Chief Barzad, but alas, as the fairies would too soon find, it was not so.

Barzad continued to torment Grass Venture, in spite of his love for the boy, and Grass Venture grew afraid of Barzad. Floating Bliss and High Wind met often away from Barzad's eye, as Kuz'Aar and Bur-duun had many times done, and all this was unknown to Barzad. Bur-duun and Kuz'Aar stayed in Dandelion Village with High Wind, their young friend, and this angered Barzad even more because he hoped all would return to normal once he was again stationed in the high seat of Thistle Town. Floating Bliss, the young thistle beauty, was never there. Bur-duun, whose love he craved, was never there. They were both away chasing dandelions and would-be dandelions in Dandelion Village, where Ben'Tork lived. Barzad felt that he was missing out, but he would not go there; that would show there was more to the lea than Thistle Town, so he pulled out his old leaf guitar and sang his loneliness into a melody nobody knew.

And far away, in Dandelion Village, Bur-duun and Kuz'Aar enjoyed their love in peace and were not afraid of showing affection in front of anyone who might see. Dandelion Village was glad to welcome Bur-duun, friend of Kuz'Aar, whom they had come to love. Bor'Tem still lived in Soggybog with her parents. And Stooping Reed had no objection, Bor'Tem being like another mother to him. Dun-Mee and Bor'Tem were now close friends. They sat together getting quietly and slowly intoxicated with the stale stem-juice of Hazy Mellow and Stooping Reed's most recent adventure—they had made a wheelie cart from old cow parsley and were using it to collect and deliver copious amounts of juice from far and wide so that the Soggybog inhabitants were ridiculously slow and nothing was being done.

This angered Wui-bur a little, but he had no control over the Soggybog fairies, who followed him not for his discipline but his young heart and sense of fun, so that when Wui-bur put his foot down, they rarely obeyed. But during this time Bor'Tem maintained a level of sobriety which exceeded that of her friends, and she put Stooping Reed to work on buttercup worship as never before. The two strove tirelessly to understand the meaning of life. What was Golden Orb's plan for them? And why had she blessed the neon yellow buttercups in her likeness?

Sometimes Dun'Mee and Sprightly-go-lightly would follow them, laughing, into the heart of the bog. The four might not return for days, until they were hunted down by a large procession and chased back to the cluster of homesteads so that all might enjoy their company. And there were parties, spontaneous and lively in nature, unlike those of Inner Lea, where Kuz'Aar's lazy personality was taking hold of the dandelions.

# FLOATING BLISS AND HIGH WIND

Bur-duun loved to lie with Kuz'Aar in the open ground, where they would wake in the morning scented of fresh grass and dewed upon. They often talked into the first light of day, and one morning the conversation moved on to Barzad.

Bur-duun grunted disagreeably at the mention of his name. 'Aw! What do you want to bring him up for? Putting me in a bad mood.'

'No!' Kuz'Aar exclaimed. 'We should forgive Barzad. He never meant to do us any harm, and we kept everything so secret. How was he supposed to know his error? I feel sorry for Barzad.'

'Barzad is arrogant and obnoxious.'

'Yes, but he loves us. And he is lonely.'

There was a pause. In that moment Bur-duun saw that Kuz'Aar was right, and she felt ashamed of her bitterness. Kuz-Aar had no anger in him, not even for Barzad, who treated him so cruelly. But if he knew then what he would later, he might have been less forgiving.

The morning grew bright. They were joined by Tu'Hob and his parents, Hob and Lyza, whose council duties were not pressing. Hob prepared breakfast as Bur-duun and Kuz'Aar washed, dressed, and chatted with Tu'Hob. Lyza played with blades of grass, circling them round his feet until his toes tickled.

'High Wind said he might come along.'

'Wonder will he bring Floating Bliss,' Bur-duun thought aloud.

'Oh, I think so,' answered Kuz'Aar. 'They're rarely apart.'

As though it were a summons, High Wind and Floating bliss came skipping round a clover corner. The older fairies sat upright and smiling, pleased that their morning's entertainment was assured. But Bur-duun was anxious to visit Bor'Tem in Soggybog where her parents would also be.

'No way! I'm staying here,' said Kuz'Aar, looking at High Wind and Floating Bliss as though to confirm his reasons. 'You go meet Bor'Tem if you like.'

Bur-duun finished her breakfast and soon was in the air drifting west, singing loudly. But half of her was sorry to leave Floating Bliss behind.

In the south, breakfast was also being served. Horaf, Shubar, Grass Venture, and Barzad gathered round a small pile of dry leaves outside Thorny Tunnel. Barzad could not hide his disappointment at Floating Bliss's absence and asked after her.

'I'd say she's gone to Dandelion Village to see High Wind.'

Barzad cursed an oath of annoyance and then said more gently, 'I can't understand why she is constantly leaving Thistle Town as though there were nothing for her here.'

'No trouble. Let her wander where she likes.'

'You know these young ones; they're always out exploring,' Shubar said, smiling, obviously with Grass Venture in mind.

Barzad, also thinking of Grass Venture, glared at him as though it were his fault, so that Grass Venture recoiled and shuddered involuntarily. Ever since Barzad's return, Grass Venture and Floating Bliss had been hiding from him. But today there was no escape; he had to tag along with his parents, though he would rather be anywhere else. He endured without fuss his parents' visits with Barzad, knowing they loved him greatly and loath to disappoint them, such was his nature. When breakfast was finally over, he said good-bye and gave to each of his parents a gentle caressing touch. Here, Barzad averted his eyes, thinking it was not appropriate to witness the affections of fairy families, and doing so made him realise he had nobody to love so dearly, nor a parent whose hand to hold. Grass Venture was a fairy who had all these things, but he could have more. *Can he not see how lovely Floating Bliss is?* thought Barzad. *She should be his, and he's about to lose her to a dandelion.*

Horaf and Shubar looked sideways at each other during the uncomfortable silence. Barzad stared into space.

'Are you okay, Barzad? You seem a bit . . .' but Barzad was miles away.

'Barzad!' Shubar said more loudly.

'What's wrong with him?' It was as though he were absent. It was no use trying to yank him from his thoughts. He was wondering what Floating Bliss was doing now. Kuz'Aar would be there, bathing in the last of the summer sun. He missed Kuz'Aar. Ben'Tork would be playing blade-whistle and dancing in that funny way. Barzad missed Ben'Tork even more. His eyes began to water, and his throat became tight. Unconsciously, he drew up his knees and hugged them.

Horaf and Shubar left him to his dark thoughts, and they were worried. They understood his loneliness for Ben'Tork but knew of nothing else that bothered him, so without his guidance they set off in search of those whom Barzad so dearly loved. There was little talk between them; they had no need for discussion. Hand in hand, they walked north until they found a pair of seeds and they rode on swiftly.

Barzad stayed behind, shivering and depressed. What had come over him at this time when all was well in the lea? Why this gloom at a time of celebration? The fairies were not united in their struggle against men, a foe some believed did not exist. Nor were they united in each other, having segregated into races rather than remain one as a species. This disharmony slowed their progression. Uulor was tired, he could see sometimes a spark of greatness in them, but in his weariness, his magic was voided so that his insight often failed him. And Barzad worried too much. He feared the winds of change, the great sweeping newness that took hold the moment they left on their long journey. But still he wanted to forget the old ways and the fairy council. He was wedged between the two, always wanting to move forward and at the same time afraid to.

Barzad came to himself and realised he was alone. *Who wants to visit with a morbid Barzad?* he thought. *I had friends here, and I scared them away.* Then he cringed at the thought of his cruelty towards Grass Venture. He knew he must make amends, so he stood up, swallowed his pride, and went off to search him out.

Grass Venture had gone far by now. Every time fairies told where they had seen him, Barzad went and found him gone from there already. Those whom Barzad met were glad to see him out among them rather than wallowing in Thorny Tunnel where dark thoughts might deepen his gloom. But the grimness had not left him as they believed; rather, it built up inside him so that upon his jealousy of High Wind he bore a burden for the fairies who lived in a region of men.

Flashbacks tormented him of the land beyond the lea where he had travelled alone in search of Bur-duun and Scuri'Boo. He remembered the feather-bills swooping and laughing around him and the huge and sweet-scented grazing-four-legs, not the least intimidated by the shadow that moved among them. In that horrible moment, Barzad realised he had seen a man. How long before the men would decide to stamp out Thistle Town? Perhaps they would never come; perhaps they would come tomorrow.

He must find Uulor and talk it through. Another fairy Barzad underestimated, he had Uulor to thank for bringing him back to the lea when he despaired of ever finding Bur-duun and Scuri'Boo, and he had Uulor to thank for finding Weedy Lea in the first place. Yes, Uulor would know what to do. Instantly he felt relieved, so now on his travels he asked after not only Grass

Venture but also Uulor. Some shrank back at this name, but seeing that Barzad was smiling, they were reassured.

Soon a procession of fairies rode through Thistle Town, half in search and half for fun. When they reached the great thistle heights, their eyes were drawn to another group riding toward them from Dandelion Village. Horaf and Shubar had returned with Ben'Tork, Kuz'Aar, Floating Bliss, and High Wind, who was always by Floating Bliss's side. The groups joined and landed where the thistles and the tall grass meet, and there a party of dance and song was begun. Kuz'Aar and Ben'Tork could see Barzad's delight at their return, and inwardly they felt guilty for having visited him so rarely. Kuz'Aar, at least, had an excuse, having been driven out of Thistle Town, but Ben'Tork's remorse was all his own, and he felt it keenly.

'Look at him,' he whispered to Kuz'Aar. 'He's giddy.'

'I bet he didn't look like that an hour ago.'

'Now I feel really bad. I wish I had visited more often.'

'And I should have stayed to help him.'

Ben'Tork looked at him sideways.

'Well . . . at least until he got somebody else.' It was a ridiculous idea. Kuz'Aar could never have stayed while their misunderstanding was unresolved, and Bur-duun would not have let him, anyway. Ben'Tork could come anytime he chose, but he remained in Dandelion Village where the parties were better while Barzad stayed behind and grew dreary in his own company.

'Well, we're here now, so come on.' Ben'Tork led, pulling out his blade-whistle. They joined the party, laughing as though nothing had been said, and Barzad never noticed them discussing him. He was too busy looking for Uulor, but Uulor was far away at the foot of Windy Hill, sleeping alone in the shady thicket. Grass Venture was with Hazy Mellow in Soggybog, so Barzad didn't find him either, and his chance to redeem himself was lost. Worse, now that the thistles were together, Barzad quickly returned to his old self, and it soon became obvious he had not exhausted that huge supply of self-esteem. While Ben'Tork and Kuz'Aar saw smiles and laughter, Floating Bliss and High Wind were not so lucky. Barzad found them talking alone, away from the main throng, and instantly he grew angry and abused them.

# GOR'TEEB

Floating Bliss and High Wind were left with a bad taste in their mouths and quickly grew bored of Barzad and his party.

'Why did we come all the way here just to be berated?' Floating Bliss asked in a tone of genuine confusion.

'Let us go to Soggybog. Grass Venture will be there,' High Wind suggested.

'Yes, Grass Venture! Now there's someone with a sense of fun. But first we must tell Barzad we're leaving.'

High Wind didn't like where this was going. 'Ah! Best not. He'll know where we are. Let's just go.'

'No, I want to . . .'

It was too late. Barzad had only gone a few steps, and Floating Bliss found him wringing his hands and muttering to himself.

'Ah! There you are hiding in the bushes, looking for innocent fairies to sneak up on.'

High Wind stood behind her, cringing.

'We're just off to Soggybog now. The welcome usually lasts a little longer there.'

Now it was Barzad who cringed.

'You won't miss us now all the dandelions have come to visit. Even Tu'Hob came here to celebrate wonderful Barzad. Oh look! Barzad's in a bad mood, better stay quiet. Oh wait! Now he's in a good mood—let's all hold hands and dance in *rings around Barzad*!'

At the last three words, Barzad's head drooped dejectedly to his knees. He had been told off by the young fairy girl with whom everyone was in love in front of the handsome dandelion boy who stole her heart. Now that Barzad's humiliation was complete, High Wind tugged nervously at her petal clothes, hoping they might escape before things got any worse. They moved away quietly, looking over their shoulders, leaving Barzad to stand alone, limp and overcome.

Grass Venture was indeed still in Soggybog with Hazy Mellow, who had him trying out nectar cocktails before offering them to the others.

'Wui-bur's not so keen on us getting intoxicated all the time, so it must be really delici—deli . . .'

'Delicious! Yes, I understand. Well, this isn't. It needs something.'

'Umm . . . nettle root, perhaps? Essence de digitalis?'

'Definitely not essence de digitalis! Do you know what that stuff does to you?'

'Oh, that only poisons men. It's perfectly safe for fairies—here, try this.' Hazy lashed copious amounts of some unrecognisable green liquid into the cup and gave it back.

'Umm. That's better. What is it?'

'If Wui-bur asks, it's sycamore sap.'

'So, where is everyone?'

'Bulrush theatre. Right! Are we ready?' Hazy finished mixing a large nutshell full. They sealed it tightly so that Stooping Reed could easily roll it down the gentle slope to the theatre and skipped off, laughing.

Hazy found him first and quietly indicated that more fuel was waiting for delivery. Stooping Reed discreetly snuck off to roll it down the hill. Grass Venture had never seen such a transaction before, and Wui-bur's reaction was great when Stooping Reed returned to loud clapping and cheering. Outsmarted again, Wui-bur buried his head in his hands, cursing mild oaths and groaning, as the excited crowd gathered round the stem juice and feasted until they were silly. Hazy Mellow brimmed with pride and wished there were more fairy girls to see him. Little did he know that the legend of Hazy Mellow was spreading throughout the lea on the lips of all the young fairies. He was no longer referred to as Stooping Reed's sidekick but as the great plant harvester who could reap the magic of stem-juice.

Bur-duun's face lit up when Floating Bliss arrived, and she excused herself from Bor'Tem, whose constant talk of buttercup worship and orbs was getting boring. She knew she had not offended because Stooping Reed instantly took the space she vacated and began questioning her on their research and how the results were going. She could hear them mumbling away enthusiastically. 'Oh, just fine, Stoop.' "Stoop" was Bor'Tem's new nickname for him. 'I think we're finally getting close to the answer.'

'Oooh! Excellent.' He huddled in closer.

*They're turning into orb-nerds, if such a thing exists,* Bur-duun thought to herself. She smiled down to Floating Bliss, who took her hand affectionately and gazed upwards in obvious adoration. High Wind stood aside and looked at them together. They got along so well, Bur-duun and Floating Bliss. It made him think if he got to know Bur-duun better, it would please Floating Bliss. He also thought it inconvenient that the fairy she most admired also had a poor relationship with Barzad. If she could just adore someone like Ben'Tork, Barzad would take it as less of an insult and give them space, but it would not turn out so.

As evening stretched on, the dandelions left Thistle Town and returned to Inner Lea. Gor'Teeb sat waiting for them, etching designs into the earth with a long thorn. She had chosen not to go to Barzad's party because she was displeased with him over his treatment of Bur-duun, but she hadn't realised how many were going until she found herself all alone. The hours passed and she grew very lonely; she had been feeling blue lately and couldn't shake herself out of it, but today was worst of all.

Eventually when the dandelions arrived, her joy was mixed with relief. Sula'Tan kissed both her cheeks, Tork shared some nettle needles left over from the party, and Ben'Tork danced a ring around her, blowing through his blade-whistle. 'You missed out! How come you never came to the party?'

'Oh! Leave her, Ben'Tork,' said Tork. 'Gor'Teeb is not so fond of Barzad as we are.' Then she effectively contradicted herself by going on to Gor'Teeb, 'Oh, he looked great, didn't he, Tu'Hob? He was really pleased with our visit.'

'That's lovely. I might sit up for a while, if anyone wants the company. I'm not really tired.'

This was an awkward moment because they were all weary and wanted to go to bed, but after a few seconds Ben'Tork piped up with feigned enthusiasm. 'Go on then! Pour me a slurp of dandelion milk.'

Gor'Teeb went to find some, and her friends shuffled off to bed. When she came back, Ben'Tork was there alone, yawning and rubbing his eyes.

'You sure you're not too tired?'

'Oh no! Not at all,' he said, not realising he had been caught yawning. It was obvious she wanted company, and he would not deny a friend in need.

'So, how was Barzad, then? I suppose I should be interested.'

'Oh! Poor Barzad,' Ben'Tork began, screwing up his face in shame. 'I feel bad 'cause he was so excited when we arrived—like he hadn't seen anyone in ages.'

'But maybe if he were kinder, fairies wouldn't keep leaving him.'

This affected Ben'Tork more than she intended. Ben'Tork was, after all, one of the fairies who left. They paused. Ben'Tork dangled his legs from their seat and watched disconsolately as they swung. Gor'Teeb followed suit.

'I should have visited more.' Ben'Tork was talking to himself now.

'He could just as easily have come to visit you, you know. If he is lonely, it's his own fault.' Gor'Teeb sounded angry.

'You are like him.' Ben'Tork laughed.

'I am not!' she said, instantly wounded.

'Oh, yes you are. You were lonely today, when we were in Thistle Town, but you would not come and join us—too stubborn. You see? Just like him.'

Gor'Teeb was taken aback. He was right. It was purely her own stubbornness that caused her loneliness today. How many times recently did she feel unhappiness of her own making? Horrified by her self-cruelty, she said nothing for a while. Eventually she began to laugh, as if a weight was lifted. 'You're right. I was foolish, but now I understand.'

'Well done.' He laughed. 'You could be so happy. "Gor'Teeb the fabulous!" Everyone loves you. You should never be lonely.'

'Sometimes I think it is I who should be the lone fairy. I feel so alone. Well, from now on I won't be!' Like a new year's resolution that was meant to last, Gor'Teeb's words would never be forgotten.

'Good for you.'

'I'll never sit alone when my friends are at a party.'

'No.'

'And I'll never let my feelings for Barzad get in the way of my joy.'

'You should visit Barzad.'

'Oh now!' She became serious. 'Don't go too far.'

'Of course you should! You visit Uulor. Many fairies would be afraid to visit Uulor, but you're not. I bet if you went to Barzad, you'd remember the good in him.'

'I suppose there is no fairy that is not good.' Ben'Tork made a little noise of appreciation as she said this. 'And if there is one with whom we are in bad relations, we could pay them a visit and soon rekindle our love.'

This was delicious to Ben'Tork, who shared himself so abundantly. *She should be more generous with her company,* he thought. *She would bring joy to others and ease her own loneliness at the same time.*

Gor'Teeb was thinking the same, and from that day onwards she toured the lea, searching out those who needed cheering up, putting smiles on gloomy faces, reuniting parted friends, and smoothing over petty arguments so that many times, when two fairies disagreed, a visit from Gor'Teeb would make it better. It was obvious with whom her first visit would be. Having said good-bye to Ben'Tork she rode a seed to Thorny Tunnel in the middle of the night when Barzad would be most alone. She shared with him her happiest thoughts, and he imparted his deep worry and gloom, which she took gladly, that his burden might be halved. He talked of the man in the pasture, of the greyness that surrounded the fairies, of how he sent Bur-duun away thinking she was in love with Scuri'Boo, and how he tried to enslave Kuz'Aar in the vain hope he could cure him of his laziness. He admitted Arthos and Tem were in Soggybog for days before he even noticed. He tried to guilt-trip Ben'Tork into staying in Thistle Town instead of moving to his parents' in Dandelion Village and he tried to disband the fairy council because he didn't believe in it. He described how stern he had been with Floating Bliss and how he had begrudged High Wind time with her; so many mistakes. His eyes were wet, and his hands covered his face. 'Oh, I'm a bad fairy. I'm selfish and wicked and cruel!'

Gor'Teeb took him in her arms and squeezed him tightly, something that had not happened to Barzad in many years.

'Barzad, most of these mistakes you made because you thought you were doing right.'

'But I have so many faults. I'm the most selfish fairy I know. I underestimate everybody. I torment Grass Venture . . .'

'So stop and save your energy for positive things.'

'But there is no positive stuff.' Barzad snivelled.

'Oh, Barzad, there are loads of positives. You love everyone so deeply. You are brave. Who was it first rode the seed? And why? You throw the biggest parties in all the lea, and look at this great city, so ostentatious! It's got Barzad written all over it.'

Barzad laughed aloud at this, and they untangled themselves.

'There you go,' she said. 'We want the old Barzad back.'

He dried his eyes with the back of his hands and gave her a grateful smile. Not the weak half-smile of someone who had just been crying but a powerful one that lit up his whole face. Well done, Gor'Teeb.

She left him and rode to Ben'Tork, who slept under a cloud of silvery mist. He looked so lovely when he slept, peaceful and innocent. A wave of love filled her heart till she was moved to tears of joy. Ben'Tork had been so good to her. She woke him.

'I've made good with Barzad.'

He nodded, eyes closed and head drooping. She had gone to him flushed with the wet August dew, whereas he was dry and inviting with hours of sleep. She thanked him for his wisdom with a crushing embrace, and her eyes were bright. Ben-Tork, still half asleep, breathed deeply and leaned more heavily on her. His arms were around her, his breath was on her neck and it felt fantastic.

# Uulor and Hidden Thicket

Uulor awoke at the foot of Windy Hill where Golden Orb had fallen. The evening air smelt of wild berries, and the season of thistle seeds was at last upon the lea. Darkness was descending quickly; the fairies would soon be fast asleep. White Orb was slim and beautiful, and Uulor felt a warm feeling as though something wonderful had happened. His first thought was of Floating Bliss and High wind, who he had been watching for some time, knowing they must eventually come together. He was glad of their joy, but the feeling was stronger than that, more intense. He knew that he must be affected in some way. Indeed, Golden Orb had plans for him, and as she lay hidden below the hazy horizon, they became real. Uulor shuffled through his mossy den in search of breakfast. Many whitetails had been here while he slept, and he ate a hearty meal of grass-seed heads and roots turned from the soil. When he finished, he went back to sift through the den as though he had lost something; he knew not that the powerful force of Golden Orb was driving him to find the joy that would consume him, for there in the thicket lay the tiny figure of a fairy baby, wide awake, gazing at the newness of the world with arms outstretched to meet his hands and eyes just like his own.

Wordlessly, Uulor took the infant to his chest and cuddled him and squeezed him and blew in his hair. White Orb was sailing across the cloudless sky. Uulor showed her to the boy and said that she was their protector at night, and she made it bright when the light of the sparkling fires was not enough.

'And sometimes she is full and round, so that only on the forest floor is the darkness complete.' They followed her from Windy Hill through the long lea until she set behind the trees of Gloomy Forest, and he pointed to the sparkling fires, those that were the brightest and named them to him.

'Vega' and the boy repeated him. Uulor named many sparkling fires, for they were out in abundance, and they too moved across the sky and set when the night was old. When the pair reached the edge of Gloomy Forest, they stood and looked into the darkness. 'This is a strange and dark place,' he said, 'and you must never go alone. Only one fairy has ever lived here, and that is Fari-bur, who now lives in Soggybog.'

From there, they swung the blades to Thistle Town, where the high weeds and the fairies slept side by side. 'This is Barzad,' he whispered. 'Most proud of all fairies, and little good it will do him.' The boy gazed a while at the frowning brow, and his first impression was one to last. Caught among the thorns was a lone thistle seed, first of the season. and they took it to ride, both together, for the boy was light. Far out to the barriers they went, and beyond, to the marshes. Sprightly-go-lightly was up already, dancing on the buttercup leaves, under the setting of the sparkling fires and the rising of Golden Orb.

'This one gets up early,' he said, and gave her a wave. Sprightly waved back, and her eyes remained on them a while. She knew little of Uulor but was sure he rarely had company, and she would be first with the news that the lone fairy had been here with a boy born new to the lea.

De'Lyza and Vi'Shay spotted Uulor next. Uulor acknowledged them in his usual silent way and continued, leaving them to wonder who his little friend was? Uulor let them talk. Soon the lea would be alive with speculation. They moved toward the fence on Windy Hill, and it was dawn before they stopped. The whitetails were up, and Scuri'Boo was in his little nest. They sat nearby and watched him dream, waiting for the full light of day.

When Golden Orb was clear above Windy Hill warmth came into the air. The boy was only born the previous night, when Golden Orb was fading, so he had not seen her before in all her beauty. Uulor explained that Golden Orb was the provider of warmth and protection during the day; he said that she made the flowers bloom and the grasses grow and that the fairies worshipped her, for she was full of glory. When she was full and high, the boy stared long at her. This hurt his eyes, and Uulor made him look away. When Scuri'Boo awoke, he saw the two, Uulor broadly grinning and proud, the boy still unable to take his eyes from Golden Orb and blinking because of it. The three sat silently while Scuri'Boo ate seeds of clover. When he was finished, they went to the whitetail warren.

Young Buck came to Scuri'Boo, and they talked, Scuri'Boo introducing his two companions. Young Buck wrinkled his nose at them. He recognised Uulor, and when he felt satisfied that he would remember the young one, he bounced away. Again the fairies were alone. The boy curled up at his father's feet, and Uulor knew he was tired. Scuri'Boo accompanied them to Uulor's den, and they laid him down on the moss and covered him with fallen leaves of bindweed. As he gazed at the boy, Uulor heaved a loving sigh. The two adults seated themselves, careful not to rumple the moss. They made childish faces at the creaseless brow and whispered soothing words to help him sleep. When they were sure he slept, they turned to each other and talked of future plans. From now on, the boy would remain with Uulor, walking with him at night, and during the day, he would sleep hidden among the moss and brambles. Uulor looked again at the little face and saw in it what was handsome in his own.

In the mornings that followed, there was much speculation throughout the lea. De'Lyza and Vi'Shay met and washed as usual, but their talk never steered from Uulor and the tiny fairy they saw with him. Sprightly also rose early and danced in the same spot, hoping she might see them once again. But they never came back to the same places; such was their way. Everywhere two fairies met or a group gathered, their talk would inevitably turn to Uulor, but they were still in the dark. The council fairies called an open meeting where everyone who wanted could attend. Some had never been to a council meeting and went out of curiosity; some attended to catch up with old friends. Some were obsessed with finding out about Uulor and the boy, and others just went because everyone else was going. Many brought stem-juice, leaf pies, or some other treat for a party afterwards, and the turnout was unprecedented. Even Barzad made his way to Inner Lea, determined to take Gor'Teeb's advice and make himself more approachable but also to discuss the issue of men in the pasture with Uulor and Scuri'Boo.

Bor'Tem, presiding, called the meeting to order in the formal way, went through the agenda, and summarised their findings so that those not on the council could keep up. All the lea gave their undivided attention, save for Barzad, who was bored already, only listened to items of his interest and examined his nails otherwise. But had he listened as everyone else did, he would have been strangely fascinated and perhaps seen in her what was so well loved by others. When Bor'Tem finished, the fairies fell silent; Uulor was on everyone's mind, and some whispered quietly to their neighbours.

'Why has Uulor not spoken?' some said. 'Perhaps there is no child. We must have been mistaken.'

But as the whispers fell to silent disappointment, Bor'Tem nodded to Uulor. He understood and raised himself slowly, that he might address the crowd.

He laughed self-consciously. 'I have something to show you all.' There was a rustle in the clump of grass beside him. Those nearest pushed back into a large circle so everyone could see him and the dark haired fairy boy who came from the grass and clutched his hand tightly. The boy looked up at Uulor, and Uulor looked down at the boy. There was rapturous applause and throwing of fairy hats into the sky. When the noise died down, Boo and Scuri'Boo were beside them, and Uulor began again.

'My friends, who among us can comprehend the workings of Golden Orb? There are some . . .' Here he glanced unconsciously at Bor'Tem and Stooping Reed. 'There are some who have striven to understand, and I believe they are none the wiser.'

Embarrassed giggles came from a cluster of marsh fairies who knew full well the work Bor'Tem put in. Bor'Tem and Stooping Reed raised their arms triumphantly, all the while laughing at themselves and their vain efforts. Uulor continued, 'Before now, before the lea, even before the long journey, I had only one friend in the world and Boo was good to me. Still, I was lonely. I never chose the lone life for myself. I doubt any of you would either. But Golden Orb had plans for me; she has plans for us all, so let us carry on and do her bidding. You see, now I understand. Golden Orb didn't mean for me to be lonely just because I am a lone. Lots of fairies live alone and aren't lonely.' His eyes met Gor'Teeb's. 'I still work at night when you're all asleep, but I feel better, and my insight is improving. Some of you are getting better too. Vi'Shay is not so tired any more, and Gor'Teeb has found her purpose.'

He looked a while at Barzad but said nothing. Barzad nodded gravely that he understood. Uulor knew about the man in the pasture; they would talk later, alone. Barzad exhaled audibly now that the weight had been lifted. Uulor went on, 'This is not what I chose, but what of it? If such are Golden Orb's plans for me, truly, I am thankful, for though I am the lonest of all fairies, I am also the happiest.' When Uulor finished, he sat down, tired, being not used to public speaking. He had aged slightly, some noticed. The multitude was silent in their gladness, and surely there was not one among them who was afraid of him.

Some elder fairies rose to shake his hand and welcome Hidden Thicket gently. He was obviously not used to crowds or loud noises. The younger ones distracted themselves with the buffet of stem juice and treats, preferring to wait rather than bombard the little newcomer, and while many backs were turned, Barzad slipped unnoticed behind Uulor and tugged urgently on his arm.

'Later!' Uulor hissed sternly, so Barzad whimpered off to find some dark spot in which to hide and wait.

Bur-duun was in wonderful tune, but her blade-whistle was not. She began the party with the familiar Lily-Pad Reel, shouting, 'Ben'Tork taught me to play!' But her notes were off, and the tune was almost unrecognisable.

'He didn't teach you to play like that!' somebody shouted from the back, which made everyone clap and whoop with laughter. Bur-duun carried on anyway, trying not to laugh for fear of losing her notes even further, and Sprightly accompanied her by dancing alongside, ignoring the dreadfulness of her playing.

Barzad could hear the fairies having fun in the distance, and it made him feel ill, so far was he from their joy. At last Uulor came. He looked exasperated but spoke patiently, seeing that Barzad was in turmoil. 'Barzad, you have to be more careful. You don't want the whole lea to know what's on your mind.'

'Is it not important?'

'Of course it's important, but you can't go scaring everyone. Not now, when things are better than ever.' Barzad was not convinced things *were* better than ever, now that men obviously owned the land. He explained these fears to Uulor and described how the energy was sucked out of everyone.

'But our energy is not being drained away. We were all weary in the beginning, and for as long as I can remember before we came here, but look at Vi'Shay. He rises with Sprightly now, and he stays up all day. He could not have done that a while ago. And in myself I've noticed changes too. I can see what's going on far better now, like I used to, long ago. For a while I was in total darkness.'

'But that's what I'm afraid of! Everything is so vague.'

'I thought so too for a long time. But if Vi'Shay can regain his strength and my insight is returning too, then surely it's the same for all fairies. So there are men beside us—what are we afraid of? If a man ever hurt a fairy before, I've never heard of it, and if our strength continues to grow, we will be able for them.'

'Will we be able for them tomorrow?'

Uulor didn't know, but he wasn't prepared to drag them all on another long journey.

'Would you leave your lovely Thistle Town?'

'I might as well. Soon I'll be the only one left!' Barzad thought regretfully at his recent behaviour, which clearly drove fairies away. The distant music stopped. Ben'Tork had rescued the fairies from Bur-duun's noise, and a few moments later came the slow, melodic tones of 'A Whisper in the Grass,' a dandelion love song popular with all the fairies. Ben'Tork was playing exceptionally well. It was one of Barzad's favourites, and he listened intently.

'It will get better, you know. We *will* be happy.' Uulor's voice brought Barzad back to their little hidey hole, far away from the music.

'What use is being happy if men are standing over us?'

'Barzad, I don't think men can even see us.'

'They can see whitetails.'

'Whitetails are far bigger than us, and they dig whole cities into the fields, and they raid vegetable gardens. Men can't help but notice them. Honestly, Barzad, we're different. We're in no danger.' The words "magic fairies" rung in his ears, but he didn't mention that to Barzad.

'Well, I suppose if there was reason to worry, you'd know about it.'

'I suppose I would. Now, let's lighten up and go back to the party?' Uulor was anxious to return to Hidden Thicket, and with the next words his tone changed. 'You know, it's not fair, you dragging me away on this of all days. You're a very selfish fairy, Barzad. But you've got to learn to deal with things instead of brooding. When you worry in such an obvious way, it makes everyone afraid. Here we are hiding away in a dark corner because Barzad has something on his mind. There are lots more constructive things you could be getting on with over there.'

Uulor nodded his head in the direction of the party. Barzad thought of Grass Venture. He still had to make amends, and this was the perfect opportunity, when all the fairies were together. Barzad felt berated and embarrassed. Uulor's words were gentle but effective.

They made their way back to the crowd and blended with the others as though they had never left, but Bor'Tem saw them return and was troubled. Perhaps she knew of Uulor's worries of another long journey, or perhaps she shared Barzad's fear of men, but whatever was on her mind, she kept it to herself, because this was not the time. Uulor went to find Hidden Thicket, leaving Barzad to stand alone. Seizing her chance, Bor'Tem skipped to him and asked how he was. Barzad eyed her suspiciously, afraid she might have seen him and Uulor and want to know what passed between them. In truth, she missed him terribly and only wanted his smile.

Barzad's only interest was to find Grass Venture, so he, in turn, moved on, leaving Bor'Tem to stand alone as he had done moments before. Grass Venture was nowhere in sight. According to Horaf, he had gone home. Shubar said he was not with her, nor was he at the buffet where Dandelion Dew sought him also. Barzad was anxious to get his apology over with and start being a better fairy, as Gor'Teeb had suggested. He quickly grew frustrated and became irritable with everyone near him. It soon transpired that Floating Bliss and High Wind were also missing. Barzad imagined the three hiding behind a clump of grass, laughing and conniving behind his back. The thought of it made him furious. He ordered a search party to find them and return them to him at Thorny Tunnel, but Horaf would not be bullied.

'Why don't you leave it, Barzad?' The fairies became quiet. Horaf was standing now.

'Leave it! He says "leave it"!' Barzad was shouting. 'Grass Venture stands on the side-lines while the only thistle girl is off cavorting with a *dandelion!* And he says to *leave it!*' Barzad turned to the crowd, waving his arms in sweeping, delirious fashion.

Tu'Hob was deeply offended at Barzad's slight. He, too, stood and met Barzad's eye.

'Is there a problem, Barzad?'

'Of course there's a problem. High Wind has no business near our thistle girl. Those daisy twins will do him fine.'

'Those daisy twins! If you're referring to my children, you will call them by their names.' Sula'Tan stood beside Tu'Hob, her leader. She could feel him shaking with outrage.

Barzad was outnumbered. Seeing that he would win no arguments here, he rode off, furious. Gor'Teeb took a seed and followed him to Thistle Town, but when she landed at his door he slammed it in her face. Unhurt, she quietly returned to the remains of the party, where some still stood in horrified embarrassment at the scene that had just taken place. Most offended of all, Horaf and Shubar mumbled to themselves in their confusion.

'"Stands on the side-lines." How dare he suggest our Grass Venture will never find a mate?'

Mumbles of agreement answered Shubar.

'Maybe if he spent more time finding a mate for himself, he would be too busy to embarrass our children.' Horaf said this.

Bur-duun hid herself momentarily so that none would notice her reaction.

Tu'Hob spoke up. 'Perhaps a few seasons on the council will give him something real to worry about.'

'For goodness sake! Don't give him any more worries.' Everyone turned to Uulor when he said this and continued to stare at him for an explanation. He could keep it a secret no longer.

'He thinks he saw a man.'

The fairies erupted in shocked cries and deep intakes of breath.

'Where? When? Did it see him?'

In their panic, the fairies noticed nothing of Grass Venture and his two friends, who came riding unconcerned around a tall bush, but Horaf and Shubar spotted them and silently ushered them home so they would be sheltered from the fear of men. Grass Venture was made to stay in their den without knowing why. Had they finally found the bad in Barzad? He dearly hoped so.

The following morning, another council meeting was held to see what could be done. The thought of Barzad making up the story about men had flitted through some minds, but Uulor believed him, and that was enough for most. Besides, not even Barzad would lie about something so serious just to get himself out of trouble. Gor'Teeb saw that in their fear of men the fairies were missing the issue between Barzad and Floating Bliss, and he had still not reconciled his differences with Grass Venture. So it was decided that she and Ben'Tork would go to Thistle Town to see how they could help. Bor'Tem was acutely aware with a pang of regret that she would be no use to Barzad in his current dilemma, but she failed to notice how close Gor'Teeb and Ben'Tork had become. She stayed behind with Uulor in the hope of finding a solution, and they decided to impose a curfew to prevent young wandering fairies being found by men.

While Bor'Tem journeyed home, she stumbled across Floating Bliss and High Wind laughing among the wild flowers of the meadow. With noise she made her presence known so as not to disturb their privacy. Their two heads peeped around a pink clump of clover and came out to join her.

'Hi.'

'Hiya.'

'Hullo,' she gently said.

'It's a nice day for a picnic. We're just going to have one.'

'That sounds lovely, High Wind, but I'm in a bit of a rush home.'

'Oh?'

'Well, you see, some fairies think they may have seen men in the area.' Bor'Tem tried to keep it light. 'It's probably nothing, but the council have decided that a curfew would be best. You won't stay out late, sure you won't?'

'If you'd prefer, we could just go back to the others,' Floating Bliss suggested.

'Maybe, Floating Bliss, you should stay here in Dandelion Village for now. Barzad is in a very bad mood, and he's looking for you both.' Instantly, Bor'Tem regretted saying it. Their faces darkened, and they looked to each other for support.

'He can keep looking.' Floating Bliss lifted her chin, but despite her show of defiance, she unconsciously reached for High Wind's hand.

'Oh, come now,' said Bor'Tem, laughing. 'It's not so bad.'

'It's always bad with Barzad.' High Wind sounded nervous. 'P—please don't tell him where we are. We just want to be left alone.'

Bor'Tem felt for them, but she felt worse for Barzad, even though it was his own fault. He didn't mean to be feared, and now he had estranged himself from these young fairies and his two best friends, Horaf and Shubar, whose son was also afraid of him.

'I won't tell a soul,' she said at last, and their relief was easy to see.

Bor'Tem left them with regret. It was not that she wanted to stay. She had too much work to do, but a bad feeling lodged itself in her mind, as though she had made some terrible mistake. She looked round to see them hiding again beneath the flowers. *Perhaps I should not have mentioned men,* she thought, but that was not it. That was not it at all.

# Missing

It was a few days before anyone noticed. With the curfew in place, nobody moved around much, so it was not until the evening Ben'Tork returned from Thistle Town and said they were not there, that the fairies wondered where Floating Bliss and High Wind had gone.

The dandelion fairies went first to Soggybog, but they had a difficult time riding their seeds in the wind and rain that wrestled with their flight. When finally soil gave way to marsh and grass to spindly reeds, the dandelions came upon Vi'Shay lolloping alone by the edges of a mossy puddle.

'Where are they?' All at once they asked, 'Where are High wind and his thistle girl?'

'Dandelion Village, I assume. Where else would they be at this time of uncertainty?' But it was not a rhetorical question, and he could see panic rising in some faces.

'Well, if she's not here, where is she?' Bur-duun's voice sounded different. There were groans and worried whispers behind her. Soon many more marshes came to see what was wrong, and the whispers became more audible.

'Okay. We must all calm down,' Wui-bur said, attempting to bring some sense to the group. 'It's probably nothing. So Floating Bliss and High Wind are gone off somewhere and we're all getting in a knot because there might be men about.'

At this, Tu'Hob's face paled and he leaned on Ben'Tork for support. It hadn't occurred to him that men might be to blame.

Wui-bur, realising his mistake, said, 'Look, they're probably just having some quiet time alone.'

'How would you feel if it were Sprightly-go-lightly?' Kuz'Aar didn't mean it as an accusation, and Wui-bur didn't take it as one.

'I would assume she was away with Stooping Reed. Would I be wrong?' This calmed some fairies, but Tu'Hob's breath would not come without gasping.

'We need to think back. When was the last time anyone saw them?' Dun-Nur said this.

Everyone thought silently until Sprightly shouted, 'The big meeting! Everyone was there.'

'Yes, but did you see them?'

'Oh! Yes, I remember!' Dandelion Dew came in. 'I asked them where Grass Venture was.' She had not intended to reveal herself so blatantly. She had told no one about her feelings for Grass Venture, not even Daisy Petal. She began to blush uncontrollably, but Daisy Petal noticed her distress and giggled behind her hand.

Vi'Shay was thinking of the embarrassing scene where Barzad made such an exhibition of himself and demanded they be brought to him. Then he thought aloud, 'Barzad might have them.'

'No. I've just been there. He was alone,' Ben'Tork said.

'Well, go back,' Kuz'Aar said. 'Talk to young Grass Venture. If he doesn't know where they are, no one does.'

'I'll go right away.' Ben'Tork took his battered seed and soon was out of sight.

'The rest of us may go home. We must be there when they return.'

'The marshes will organise our own search.' Wui-bur spoke loudly to their turned backs. 'As soon as we know anything, we'll go straight to Dandelion Village. We will even ride seeds there because it is so urgent.'

The fairies separated, and Kuz'Aar led the dandelions home. It was a long journey, and some were too worried to concentrate on their riding. This led to a few crashes. In one incident, Bud-duun collided with Gor'Teeb's seed, causing her to fall to the ground. The fairies screamed in panic, but her injury was only minor.

Ben'Tork had no such dramas. His swift flight took him smoothly to Horaf's door within minutes. Grass Venture was bored senseless and delighted with the visitor, but it was not a happy Ben'Tork who came to the door. The mood quickly became serious. Ben'Tork explained what was afoot.

'Oh, I thought you had come to say the curfew was over.'

'No, I'm afraid it's still very much in place and likely to stay until we find out what happened to them.'

'You see,' Horaf began telling Grass Venture, 'there is a reason for the curfew, a reason we didn't tell you.'

'There are men,' said Shubar. 'Just over there, beyond the thistles, in the pasture.'

'We dandelions are beginning to believe men may have taken them.' Ben'Tork said this, and then there was silence.

Grass Venture reeled a little and sat back. He was going to retch. Horaf and Shubar eyed each other worriedly.

'When were they last seen?' Shubar asked.

'Dandelion Dew says she saw them at the big meeting.'

'Yes, we saw them there. But, well, you know how Barzad was. We sent them off before he saw them.'

'I don't think anyone has seen them since. Grass Venture, do you know anything?'

Horaf took the boy's shoulders and looked hard into his face. No. He knew nothing.

'We got separated on the way home. I went on ahead.'

'Curse of the orbs!' Ben'Tork had thought he would go home with something positive, but this was a real disappointment.

'What are we to do now?' Shubar went also to Grass Venture and rubbed his shoulder. He coughed and spluttered a little and then recovered, standing straight.

'We must go to Barzad,' said Ben'Tork. 'He'll know what to do.'

The parents hesitated, Barzad's recent behaviour still fresh in their minds. Grass Venture looked up at them to see their reaction. Ben'Tork could see they were united in their fear of him and sought to reassure them.

'Don't worry about all that unpleasantness back at the meeting. I talked to him. It'll be okay.'

Still they were anxious, but he urged them gently onwards to Barzad's door.

Barzad did not expect to see Ben'Tork again so soon, especially with Grass Venture by his side.

'Come in, come in,' he mumbled, leaving the door open and standing back that they might pass.

'Floating Bliss and High Wind are gone.'

'Okay. I'll talk to them when they get back, but to you, Grass Venture, I also owe an apology.'

'No! They're gone . . . gone missing.'

Barzad thought they had come to settle their differences. This other reason was a shock, but here was Grass Venture. Barzad would not lose a second chance to make amends. Ben'Tork, Horaf, and Shubar discussed loudly and pragmatically what should be done while Barzad sat in a dark corner with Grass Venture, explaining himself as best he could. The new, improved Barzad, who spoke softly and respectfully, took Grass Venture by surprise. He listened as Barzad admitted his error and apologised profusely. Ben'Tork saw this also, though he said nothing to Horaf and Shubar. Perhaps he and Gor'Teeb had made an impression. They stopped talking suddenly, which Barzad didn't notice in time to prevent the last words of his apology being heard. But as for what else was said, neither Barzad nor Grass Venture enlightened them.

'We think we should hold another meeting,' Horaf spoke stiffly to Barzad. His body language still showed a lack of forgiveness, 'a meeting for the whole lea. We can tell everyone, all at once, and start the search straight away.'

'But that would attract the men's attention, and they might take someone else.' Barzad suggested.

'Only if they see us,' said Ben'Tork brightly, and he exalted inwardly at this next idea. 'You see, we meet in stealth, when White Orb is risen and the men have returned to . . . to wherever it is men go at night.'

'Excellent, but wait!' said Barzad. 'We do it in groups. No meandering in twos and threes. The marshes will go at once all together, and we thistles, at once all together, meeting in Inner Lea, close to everyone. If we go in groups, no one will go missing.'

'The marshes have already started looking. They could be spread all over by now,' Ben'Tork said darkly.

'Awh! Damn them stupid marshes!' Barzad shouted. Then he collected himself. What could the marshes do but go looking immediately? It was exactly what Barzad wanted to do. Barzad took his stem horn and blew loudly so all Thistle Town awoke. Then, turning to Ben'Tork, he said, 'We will ride now to Inner Lea, when the men are away, and we will be ready before morning.'

Within minutes all Thistle Town were skyward, heading towards Dandelion Village, determined and unflinching in the dark midnight air.

Boo was never one to obey the rules, so as evening drew towards curfew, she donned her favourite petal hat and made for the outskirts, where Uulor should just be rising. But Uulor was already gone to Inner Lea, where the panic was spreading, and Boo would not find him until much later, so she was the last to know what was afoot. Instead, she wandered a while from there to Inner Lea, regardless of the curfew, until she heard noises and thought there must be a party on. There she found Uulor, whose face was not gleeful but dark and lined with the horror of the day. Scuri'Boo also arrived, but he had already been told. Now everyone knew. The marshes had searched all day, and there was not a sign of them.

Tu'Hob composed himself and made to speak to the multitude, but words failed him, and he collapsed into a pitiful heap on the ground. Ben'Tork took over.

'The marshes have looked. They are not there, nor are they here in their home. They are not in Thistle Town, nor are they rambling around in between; Uulor made sure of that. So they are not anywhere in the lea. This we know.'

Bur-duun and Kuz'Aar took each other's hands and held together in a painful grip.

Ben'Tork went on. 'We fear the feather-bills, but they would not harm us so cruelly, and the squealing-four-legs have no use for us. The hopping greens and the high weeds love us, so it was none of those. We are sure of it. This can only be the work of men.'

Only three fairies disagreed. Vi'Shay didn't believe in men. He thought the two would come home the next day, and he laughed inwardly at the joy their return would bring, but he was wrong. Barzad went cold at the thought of the man in the pasture, but he saw his own part in their disappearance. Perhaps if he had tormented them less, they would not have been alone to be taken. He spoke this, brave Barzad, expecting to be universally hated, but the fairies pooh-poohed his fears, all except Bor'Tem, and she was silent.

'We must never separate nor go alone,' continued Ben'Tork. He looked long at Scuri'Boo, who had decided already; he would go and live with Uulor and his brother. Boo would come too.

'And the curfew is a bad idea. Why go to bed when the men do? We should be out with White Orb. Let night be our new day.' At this, Stooping Reed slumped in disappointment. How would he enjoy the rays of Golden Orb, and what research would he get done at night? He looked at Bor'Tem to meet her eye, but she seemed strangely preoccupied. and still she was silent.

'This is the time for fairies to be strong. We've come all this way.' Here there was a pause while Uulor was appreciated. It didn't happen often, and he felt it.

'We've come all this way, and if we remained in the last place, if we remained to await what troubles tomorrow might bring, they would have come from men. Why do they chase us so? Let us never find out. Let us hide ourselves from men and search the four corners of the lea until we find some clue how they were taken.'

Vi'Shay raised his hand. 'Surely if men had simply walked in and stolen them, we would have seen.'

This caused a stir. Some fairies noisily affirmed his idea, some disagreed, but still, Bor'Tem was silent and her head was bent low.

'Vi'Shay' said Ben'Tork, 'you don't believe in men. That's obvious.'

'No, I don't.'

'Well . . . how much proof do you need?' This silenced the fairies. Some more held hands, and Ben'Tork continued.

'We must not wander around the lea searching. We must be strategic and disciplined, or we will lose more. Those of you who sleep out in the open must hide yourselves. Bur-duun, Scuri'Boo, and Uulor can show you how to make your homes hard to find, and the thistles must be careful. They live nearest the men, but they are also nearest the whitetails, and that is good.' Barzad thought with a pang of regret how he had treated the whitetails. Dismissing their request to dig beside Thistle Town, and now he was glad they did it anyway, thanks to Scuri'Boo.

The fairies discussed their options long into the cold night. Some had constructive ideas, some were too panicked to think straight, and all the while Bor'Tem spoke not a syllable.

She knew what had happened to them. She was the last to see them. They as good as told her, but not until now did she understand. Too afraid to repeat those words she spoke when last she met them; instead they rang in her ears like giant church bells. Louder and louder they grew, enhancing the accusation, torturing Bor'Tem with guilt: 'I won't tell a soul.'

They had run away.

# THE SEARCH

The enormity of Bor'Tem's mistake stayed with her while the other fairies prayed in vain and hid in dark places plotting against men. What could she do next? She could not bring herself to speak to anyone, nor could she sit around waiting for the elopers to return. Only one option remained, and that was most unthinkable of all, she must go in secret to the great wide world beyond the lea and search for them alone, leaving those behind to think she had also been taken, so they would weary themselves with needless worry of men, while she might search forever and never find them.

Not far away, Bur-duun also wrung her hands. She could not be at peace, and Kuz'Aar was at a loss to console her, so she snuck out while he fidgeted in sleep and found her way to Bor'Tem. When Bor'Tem saw her sister's disconsolate face, she could hide her secret no longer and the whole sorry affair spilt out before she could stop it. Almost incoherently, she told 'It's all my fault. They were avoiding Barzad, so I promised to tell no one where they were. You see? There are no men—they've run away!'

Bur-duun held her close and whispered gently, 'Shh. That's not your fault. I see it now. You've done nothing wrong.'

'Oh, but I have. They practically told me they were running away, and I didn't understand.'

'Be calm now, Bor'Tem. Take a deep breath. What words did they use to tell you?'

'They said they just wanted to be left alone.'

'Well now, how could you have known they meant to run away?'

'It was the way they said it. They were avoiding Barzad, but I said he was looking for them. You should have seen their faces. They were afraid of him . . .'

'I'll bet they were. You see, it's all Barzad's fault, not yours. The good news is that men haven't got them. We'll find them.'

Bor'Tem's breath became less erratic. She could see the sense in Bur-duun's words, but she loved Barzad dearly and would not have him blamed. Bur-duun would.

'Early in the morning we will tell everyone the good news. But first you rest.' Bur-duun laid her gently down. Immediately, Bor'Tem fell into exhausted sleep. As her breath became rhythmic, Bur-duun turned towards Thistle Town and her eyes were dark.

All Thistle Town was quiet but for the sound of dry thistle heads rustling in gentle breeze. Darkness everywhere, and deeper dark in the shadows; Barzad was asleep. Bur-duun stood over him, staring, thinking how she abhorred him and his ugly soul, how the lea would be better off without him. He looked peaceful in his sleep, as though nothing were wrong. How dare he? She despised him for it. In one movement she grabbed him violently so that he was suddenly awake.

'It was you!'

'Uhhh?'

'It was you. There are no men—they ran away, and you drove them to it.'

'Wait now . . . Bur-duun.'

Her hands were around Barzad's neck, choking him. 'I saw a man. I know I did . . .'

'You're lying!'

'Why would I lie about a thing like that?'

'To cover up your guilt. They were afraid of you. You hear me? You drove them away.' Bur-duun's voice was broken and full of emotion. Now it failed her completely. In that horrible moment Barzad realised at last who were the parents of Floating Bliss, and he saw the magnitude of his error. A tidal wave of guilt swept over Barzad as Bur-duun lay in a broken heap on the floor. He had done this to her whom he loved. He knew not how to fix it, but Bur-duun saw his remorse and sought to exploit it. She composed herself, remained quiet until her mind was clear and when she knew she could trust herself, she spoke.

'You will fix this, Barzad, just as you left the lea to find Scuri'Boo and me. Remember when you sent us to go and live in dark tunnels with the whitetails? I thought your cruelty had reached its limits then, but now I see. You can stoop to even greater depths. When Ben'Tork spoke of this, when he said they were gone, you said yourself it was your fault, but they all said no. They still believed your "men" story. Well, it *is* your fault.'

Barzad buried his head deep in his arms and groaned, but she went on. 'You will go beyond the lea, and you will not return until you find them. I will explain that there are no men, just your lies, and that you are gone to find them. You will have no shame to hide because in the morning when I tell them, you will already be gone.' And she turned from him, as many others would do.

A draught invaded Thorny Tunnel as Bur-duun stepped into the cold night. Barzad stood unsteadily and looked around, dry eyed. No use crying now, he had lost everything of his own doing. Why should Bur-duun have sympathy for his mistakes? His leaf guitar was all he took. It clanged noisily as he dangled it over his shoulder on his way out; the sound would never be heard in Thistle Town again.

Bor'Tem awoke refreshed. It felt like the first time she had slept in years. Outside, she heard the hustle and bustle of fairies moving about. Bur-duun had already spread the word. Another meeting was to take place in Dandelion Village, and most marshes had already arrived. The thistles were making their way on the few seeds left unbattered by autumn winds, for summer had been and gone. By the time Bor'Tem's breakfast was done, they were all spilling into Dandelion Village like grains of sand in an hourglass—all, that is, except one.

When they were settled, Bur-duun spoke. 'We are gathered again, but this time a glimmer of hope can be shared. We have found the truth of it. There are no men.'

This caused a great stir among the fairies, who could not contain themselves. With the fear of men assuaged, the curfew would be over and so there was celebration except in the heart of Uulor, who knew the men were real.

'Floating Bliss and High Wind have not been captured by men, nor by any creature of the lea. They preferred to live alone, where none might know of their welfare, than to endure Barzad's incessant harassment, so they ran away.'

There was silence and holding of hands. Bor'Tem lowered her head. Her own fault in their disappearance had not been mentioned, which made her feel even more sorry for Barzad. Bur-duun continued, 'I'm sure that, great as Barzad's capacity is for cruelty, he did not intend this, so he will atone for his guilt. He has gone beyond the lea, and he will not return until he finds them.' Her words were calm, but Bor'Tem saw her knuckles were white and her fists were clenched. Bor'Tem cried inwardly at Barzad's departure. How long would he be gone? And if the lovers returned without him, how would he ever be found? She thought of following him herself, but her idea was interrupted by the thistles.

'What will become of Thistle Town?' asked Horaf loudly.

'The thistles are not destitute of great minds; what of your own, Horaf?' This was from Gor'Teeb.

'Me? I have no experience for such things.'

'But you and Shubar are greatly loved. Between the two of you, Thistle Town would do all right.' This made Grass Venture very proud indeed.

'It's not about love. Look at Wui-bur over there. He is loved also, but the marshes laugh at him and only obey when they choose.'

'Horaf's right,' Wui-bur shouted over the exclamations. 'I have about as much control over the marshes as Hazy Mellow has over his legs.'

Some marshes giggled at this in a corner. In their midst, Hazy Mellow was triumphant in his intoxication. The fairies were distracted and looked towards them until a tiny voice spoke unhindered. 'Everyone listens to the wise words of Bor'Tem.'

It was Hidden Thicket. Stooping Reed found Bor'Tem's eye and she his; their hearts sank together, but Hidden Thicket was right.

And so it was agreed. From that day forth, Bor'Tem would guide Thistle Town until Barzad returned. And what a different place it would be without Barzad, the moody, flamboyant leader they loved so well, and young Floating Bliss, who possessed their hearts! And what of buttercup worship and Golden Orb? Stooping Reed would be left to study alone. The curfew over, now all fairies could enjoy the brightness of day, but for Stooping Reed this would be coupled with the loss of Bor'Tem, who must go to live in Thistle Town, the place devoid of buttercups she chose to leave. In Soggybog they would have to fare as best they could without her. Wui-bur would feel keenly the loss of her guidance. And what of Dandelion Village? Bereft of High Wind, Tu'Hob was all but lifeless, so Ben'Tork took over the duty of leadership. But he would rather be with Gor'Teeb. And for the lones, there was also work to be done. Uulor and Scuri'Boo met without word and vacated quietly that they might discuss the future of fairies in a world of men—for men there were indeed, even if only they believed.

Boo and Hidden Thicket found themselves alone as the crowds dispersed.

'Well, what do you think of that, Thicket? It's a mess for sure,' said Boo. Hidden Thicket thought to himself, *if Barzad could see the chaos he left behind, perhaps it would cure his pride.*

The two set off home to think quietly. On their way, they met a group of thistles discussing what was to be done.

'We will look first in the pasture,' Horaf was saying. 'And we can enlist the help of the whitetails.' Enthusiastic cheers followed. Boo and Hidden Thicket left them to it.

Uulor greeted them as they squeezed into his tiny den.

'Well, now the curfew's over, I can go live by the speedwell again,' said Boo.

'And I wouldn't mind a visit with the whitetails. They might know something about Floating Bliss and High Wind,' Scuri'Boo answered.

'You're lucky,' said Hidden Thicket. 'The thistles are going there. We found out along the way.'

Uulor exalted at the peace and quiet he would soon enjoy. It was not that his welcome was short lived, but his den was tiny and the four were overcrowded. When they had eaten, Scuri'Boo left for Thistle Town that he might guide Horaf and his friends to the whitetail city. Boo returned to her speedwell patch. Uulor and Hidden Thicket crawled further into their nest to sleep.

It had been a long day, but the night in Thistle Town had only started. Relief was in the air. The lovers had not been taken by men, and Barzad would soon have them back. In the meantime Bor'Tem belonged to Thistle Town, and for that they were grateful.

A fabulous party was begun and all fairies were invited, but to Soggybog especially a warm hand was extended, that they might say farewell to Bor'Tem. She was surrounded through the night and though she had neither Gor'Teeb's beauty nor Ben'Tork's charisma she was more than comfortable with the attention lavished upon her. Never far away were her parents and Bur-duun, who made no attempt to hide her trepidation at the thought of her sister returning to Thistle Town, where Barzad had treated them all so cruelly.

# Beyond the Lea

Far away from celebrations and far from the whitetail pasture, deep beneath a patch of blooming violets where no creature would think to push his snout, two fairies lay sleeping in exhausted embrace. Their petal clothes were long gone, blown in the wind and rent by briars until there was nothing left but skin, pale with the fear of their actions. To elope is no small feat for a fairy.

It was midday but dark still under the canopy of branches, and the forest floor was dry and crisp with the fallen leaves of autumn. The fairies lay as if in comas while around them the forest folk looked on in awestruck amazement; it was a long time since a fairy had been seen in this part of the woods.

'What should we do?' asked the oak sapling.

'Let's wake them up!' said his friend the birch.

'We should give them a poke,' suggested the bramble, extending a prickly branch towards them.

'Certainly not! Cruel Bramble.' The branch was retracted obediently. Moss continued, 'We should be soft to them.'

'Should we introduce ourselves?' asked the wood mushrooms.

'That might scare them away.'

'We could just talk to ourselves and pretend not to notice them,' said the bramble.

'Will you still pretend not to notice when they pull off your petals and eat them?' said Birch with a tone of sarcasm.

'Oh, that's just a myth,' said Moss. 'They only eat petals that have fallen, and besides . . .'

'Shhh, look!' A tiny white fairy leg was moving. High Wind sat up and rubbed his eyes. Floating Bliss awoke also, and yawned loudly.

Bramble saw that they were naked, so he shook in the gentle breeze. Some petals fell near the fairies, who skilfully folded them into garments and clothed themselves. Birch winked at Bramble, who brimmed inwardly with joy that he had pulled it off so well, for the fairies were still unaware of their audience. And all the while, the weeds watched and nudged each other every time the fairies did something new. Once they bathed in a puddle, they ate silently on spent petals. and when they talked, the weeds listened. In this way the weeds discovered how the fairies arrived and where they came from. They were not long putting the puzzle together. The fairies were in love; they left their home to be together and came to hide in the forest.

After several days the weeds grew less shy and became emboldened. The oak sapling spoke in his most regal voice. 'Welcome to the fairies, most blessed of all creatures.'

'Yes, welcome indeed,' they all chimed in. Floating Bliss and High Wind were instantly heartened by their kind words.

'We've come to live in the forest, if that's okay.'

'That's wonderful,' someone cheered.

'We'd love to have you.' This came from Birch, whose silver branches swayed softly that he might get a better look. The forest folk cheered, and above their heads the mighty branches creaked in shared consent.

'You'll need somewhere with lots of petals to eat,' said the mushrooms, thinking back on what they had seen over the last few days.

'And somewhere to lie.'

'And a puddle to bathe.'

'There is a stream, you know, just over that mound there.' The bramble pointed a toothed branch so that everyone could see. And so there was. The fairies found a small slope upwards and a tiny trickle of water, swift but shallow. Nearby cavernous hollows yawned where trunks gave way to roots of evergreen, almost hidden from view and floored with pine needles, softened with age. And every which way about them were dotted fallen leaves and petals to eat. It was more than just a sunken den in which to hide, it was the perfect place to live; where men may never come and Barzad may never find them.

The months pressed on in Weedy Lea, the weather turned colder, winter set in, the pasture was white with snow, and the whitetails could rarely be seen. Scuri'Boo and his friends wandered the pasture, but their search grew frustrated and one by one they returned to the lea, disheartened and cold. Grass Venture missed the company of Stooping Reed and Hazy Mellow, so he left first. Shubar soon followed, and not long after, Horaf grew useless with homesickness and retraced alone the steps he had at first taken full of hope.

Scuri'Boo, Uulor, Bur-duun, and Kuz'Aar were all that remained, and they were determined, but the wearisome days grew darker, frostier, and more hopeless until they knew they must return empty handed.

'We can't stay here forever,' Uulor at last sighed.

'It's not safe. One fairy might hide, but a group could be seen,' suggested Scuri'Boo.

'Seen by whom? There are no men, I told you,' Bur-duun said almost happily.

'Oh, Bur-duun, there are men,' said Uulor. 'Where do you think the fences come from? And all those straight lines over there?'

'And those huge poles and that enormous thing over there? You think nature made that?' Scuri'Boo was pointing to a pylon. There was a pause during which Kuz'Aar and Bur-duun slowly came to believe.

'If this is men country, we shouldn't stay,' said Kuz'Aar, and he looked at Bur-duun deeply. She knew what he was really saying.

'Wherever the whitetails are, they are not in the pasture. Your parents will need you too.'

'But the whitetails will know what to do. They can help. Let's keep looking just another little while until we find them,' Bur-duun pleaded desperately.

Uulor took her by her free hand. The other was in Kuz'Aar's. Gently he explained, 'Every day the snow covers more ground so their burrows are harder to find. I can stay, but you should all go home. It's no use everyone being here.' He believed the lone fairy should take the responsibility.

'But Hidden Thicket is at home. I will stay.' Scuri'Boo said this, and in the silence that followed they all agreed. Uulor felt for poor Scuri'Boo, alone in the frozen pasture all the dreary winter, with no company but the odd feather-bill braving the cold and the lifeless flakes of snow. He must stay and search, no matter how cold the cold, how hard the frost.

They ate together, one last time, a meal of frosted bites, huddled in the shade of a clump of vegetation where the cold was less severe. When the time came to part ways, they soberly did, leaving Scuri'Boo behind but undaunted. He had been here before, and he would soon find the whitetails and enlist their help, but this time it was different. In all his life he had never felt so utterly alone, and he thought to himself as he watched his friends disappear down the hill of the pasture, *Am I the 'lonest of us all'? Uulor has Boo, and Gor'Teeb has Ben'Tork. I alone am without a mate and unlikely to find one. Surely I must be the lonest of us all?*

The melting snow dripped as beads of silver onto frozen soil, hard as the rocks beneath. Thorny Tunnel had slowly disappeared under a roof of brambles grown bold through months of neglect. Uulor realised, his last ray of hope gone, that Barzad had not returned; so he had not found the lovers either. This made their empty-handed return all the more hard to bear. Bur-duun eyed Uulor and saw what he was thinking.

'Scuri'Boo will return a hero. He will bring them back.' She said this, but Uulor was not encouraged.

Kuz'Aar was filled with self-loathing. It was all Barzad's fault, but he hated himself even more for being so stupid, so gullible. 'We should forgive Barzad,' he remembered telling Bur-duun. 'He never meant us any harm.' Kuz'Aar believed it once, but now he believed the opposite. Barzad always treated him differently, enslaved him while everyone else played and forced him away from Bur-duun so Barzad could have her all to himself. Now Floating Bliss, the product of their love, was gone. Of course he meant it. He did it out of jealousy. A wave of hatred swept over Kuz'Aar, something no fairy had felt before and it frightened him.

A meeting was called, and all the fairies attended. The news quickly spread that the searchers had returned empty handed, and there grew the awful possibility that Floating Bliss and High Wind might never return. Kuz'Aar was not shy to point the finger of blame. He voiced loudly that Barzad was at fault. 'Barzad has brought this on us all. Barzad must not return!'

And quietly he said to Grass Venture when no one else could hear, 'We must rise up against Barzad if ever he returns. We must annihilate him.' Grass Venture heard and was silent.

If Uulor was beside them, he noticed nothing. He was focused on Tu'Hob, who had aged terribly in the winter months of their absence. Tu'Hob worried for High Wind and ate so little that his strength waned. It was affecting his work on the council, Bor'Tem had said. He easily lost concentration. Was he losing his mind? This made Uulor afraid. It was he, Uulor, who had brought them to this place. What if it was the wrong place? The thought had occurred to him before, and now it came with renewed vigour. Perhaps the long journey was not over after all.

Grass Venture slipped away from the meeting to find his adoring Dandelion Dew. She would listen and do what he said unconditionally. Kuz'Aar would have his revolt. Grass Venture was sure.

# Scuri'Boo and the Whitetails

Bor'Tem cleared up the last of her notes and folded them into a seed pod, the tools of her trade as honorary chief of Thistle Town. The seedcase was cumbersome to carry as she made her way, tired and damp, in the March rain. Barzad never needed a case, she thought. It was all in his head, that great big mine of information. What Barzad knew from experience, she had to study. Leading a town of fairies was hard work. Is it any wonder that even Barzad made a few mistakes? Tem and Arthos had pleaded with her to come on a picnic. Bur-duun would be there, they said. It was ages since they all spent time together, but she had too much work on. She felt like she was swimming in water way too deep, but she had to press on and give Barzad something to be proud of if he ever returned. Now she felt horribly lonely for him. Sometimes it helped to spend time with Ben'Tork; he talked of Barzad always, but he was with Gor'Teeb now, snuggling in some corner. Bor'Tem was not bitter, but she began to wonder at their getting together.

*Gor'Teeb and Ben'Tork were no different to me all our adult lives; now they are lovers. What changed? And why do I have to fall in love with the one I can't have? Even Uulor has a mate. Perhaps he is not the lone fairy after all. Is it I?* The thought made her shudder. Such a magnitude of responsibility would put leading Thistle Town in the shade. To live forever a life of solitude so that others would find peace and happiness, it was too much to ask of anyone. Then she thought of Uulor. Had she not expected it of him for years? It was common knowledge that Uulor hated being the one. He was forced into it. Bor'Tem remembered how the council met and discussed his fate as though he were not among them. They were authoritative, even condescending. Had the most learned misinterpreted the fairy lore and coerced Uulor into a role he could not fulfil? Uulor pleaded with them that night, told them 'It is not I.' but their voices were louder, and eventually he did what he was told. After all, it was Uulor insisted they leave the old place and embark on their long journey, so they listened and believed. He led them to the lea, still they believed. But nothing in the fairy lore told of a long journey, just that a lone fairy would lead them beyond their limitations and eventually they would reclaim this world from men and take it for themselves. They would mend it and share it gladly with all living things, not destroy it as the men had done.

She could air her doubts to Tu'Hob, chief speaker of the council, but lately he seemed distracted and he had deteriorated even more. High Wind's disappearance had taken its toll on him. Now his face was aged with lines, and there was gauntness where before was the bright face of high spirits. He rarely rose until late in the morning and retired before dark, having eaten almost nothing. He spoke of High Wind constantly, sometimes raving. High Wind would be full grown by now, and Tu'Hob ached to see him again in the full bloom of adulthood. Bor'Tem plodded on, seedcase in hand, so concerned with Tu'Hob and her own fears that she passed closely where Kuz'Aar and his band of rebels met in secret and watched her go by.

'She's gone now,' Grass Venture whispered, peering over a dandelion leaf. He turned to his comrades and settled among them again. There were Kuz'Aar and Bur-duun, whose motives were obvious. Boo still resented Barzad for sending Scuri'Boo away, and Grass Venture loathed Barzad's penchant for persecution. Dandelion Dew, the only one with nothing against Barzad, was only there because she followed Grass Venture in all that he did.

Kuz'Aar picked up where they left off. 'Barzad will be bored by now. He will return soon a failure and still expect a hero's welcome. We must be already gone.'

'No,' said Boo. 'What of my Scuri, all alone in the pasture with those great big beasts grazing the grass around him?' Boo wrung her hands. Bur-duun gently held her in her arms.

'Don't cry, Boo. Scuri'Boo will be safe. I'm sure of it.'

'Bur-duun's right,' said Kuz'Aar. 'He'll be with the whitetails by now. They'll get him back soon, and the young ones too. All will be well, but we must be ready to leave the moment they return.'

Kuz'Aar's confidence was not catching. Everyone disagreed. Even if they did return—and it was looking unlikely—at best they would be exhausted from their ordeal and would need lots of time to recover before embarking on another long journey. Kuz'Aar was disappointed, but the others were right. And so it was through the winter months. The rebellion gained urgency but not momentum, for nothing could be done until after, and if, the missing fairies returned.

Spending a whole winter with little sustenance is tough on anyone, and Tu'Hob's face grew grey with the pallor of death. All the lea were hopeless, and the weeds noticed the change. But in the pasture there was a ray of hope. March winds blow fiercely, and the pickings are slim for whitetails, but what fear have they with a fairy in their midst? Scuri'Boo had found them at last, emerging in warm, thick coats. They told him of their winter, showed him to the new generation, and explained where the four-legs grazed. He wondered at their absence, but they had not yet come out to grass. Further down the warren, chief Big Buck arranged his transport back to Weedy Lea. 'The whitetails will continue searching the pasture from now on. It is time for you, Scuri'Boo, to return to your friends. Maybe your forest fairy could seek them among the mighty oaks.'

'Gloomy Forest.' Scuri'Boo sighed. 'I never even thought to look there; it would be the perfect place. Barzad would never go there.'

'Well, there's nowhere else they could be. Otherwise we would have found them,' said Little Doe, who liked to forage in the cover of the forest.

'But we could have mistaken them for other fairies who were not lost,' answered Young Buck.

'Oh no. No, no, no. You would not mistake these fairies for another. You see, these two fairies are very special. Wherever they go there is gladness, and they are the most handsome fairies that ever there were . . .' Scuri'Boo had to stop himself. Tears were coming.

'But all fairies are handsome and bring gladness.'

'It's the magic,' said that tiny voice again—the same voice that spoke to Uulor.

'Dainty Nibble is right,' said Bounding Haunches. 'We can still see an improvement in our pelts. They are thick and healthy where before they were prone to disease. You fairies have given us the gift of strength. There is blessing and wonderment all around you. How can you not see it?'

'Perhaps we should not press him too hard,' Little Doe interrupted, seeing the effect of their words on Scuri'Boo.

'Oh, sorry, Sc'Boo,' Bounding Haunches said breathlessly. He was overexcited. Winter was long and dreary for the whitetails, and Bounding Haunches was glad a fairy had returned to brighten up their world.

'No worries. I'm okay.' Scuri'Boo smiled behind watering eyes. Chief Big Buck had come to send him home.

'We thought at first men took our friends. Now that we know the truth, we will not stay hidden. And we will visit often.' Scuri'Boo climbed atop Young Buck, and they moved to the warren mouth. They turned, waved briefly, and were answered by loud cheering and boisterousness. They left. The whitetails crammed the entrance and looked a long while after as their friends grew smaller in the distance.

Boo slept all afternoon. The morning's meeting had given her some respite from her fear for Scuri'Boo. *Will he ever come back?* she thought. Right now, all she wanted was to see his face again, with or without the young elopers. How long could she keep the fairies from leaving Weedy Lea? They were anxious to go. Would they leave without him? Would he get stuck here with Barzad? Worse, would he get stuck here alone? No. She would never leave without him, even if it meant waiting by herself—but she might wait forever and he might never return. Nausea woke her. She emerged bleary eyed from her hideout to the clamour of a fairy party. *What could be good about the day?* she thought, disgruntled, squeezing through the throng of skipping legs and dancing partners.

Finding no way past them, she was pushed and forced inside their thick, heaving circle and fell upon her knees. At last someone noticed and took her hand. She raised herself up and looked into the face of her hero. It was Scuri'Boo.

# RETURN

The mountainous air was sharp with spring scent. High Wind recognised none of the wild plants from the lea here in the dark wood, where dandelions and thistles seldom grew. Everything was new to him; every day a new beginning, a voyage of discovery. His only constant lay still asleep, dreaming in silent contentment. True, they were lonely, but there was no doubt they had made the right decision. Homesickness was nothing compared to the nausea of worry, and that was something they left all traces of behind. No Barzad towering over them, no hiding in the long grass, afraid he might see; free at last to do as they pleased, they skipped and danced so the trees and woodland flowers rejoiced in their company. Every day was one of hyperactive merriment. Now with fresh eyes they understood what they had never noticed in the lea; gone was the greyness of which Barzad whispered. Their world was vibrant. They felt alive, energised, coloured in.

A movement in the woods; Floating Bliss stirred and woke. High Wind was not about. 'Get some for me!' she shouted, knowing he would be rummaging for breakfast; another movement in the woods, and a giggle.

'I can hear you laughing! C'mon, I'm starving.' But High wind did not answer and the laughing ceased. The woodland flowers were starting to open. Floating Bliss distracted herself by talking to them while she washed and waited.

'High Wind is very slow today. I should be helping him find food.'

'There is less because other fairy comes and eats during the night,' said a budding spring bulb.

'No he doesn't. High Wind eats when I do.'

'Not him, *other* fairy . . .' a flower began, but High Wind had returned.

'Slim pickings, I'm afraid.' he sighed, pouring a few pine needles onto the forest floor.

'That's plenty. Look, we got neighbours.' Floating Bliss pointed, and the flowers raised their heads slightly, to be seen. But as they did, a movement beneath them startled the lovers and out came a tiny fairy baby, unclothed and scented of resin. He looked around him, noticed the flowers, skipped lightly to his parents, and raised himself on wings that fluttered easily. There he hovered, searching, discovering while High Wind and Floating Bliss were silent and stupefied. In time they would find their voices and tell him of the world, of Weedy Lea and the fairies they left behind. In time they would talk of the fairy lore, of Uulor, even of Barzad and why they left, but first they would enjoy this moment, the greatest of their lives.

In Weedy Lea, Scuri'Boo was empty handed but not beaten. The whitetails would continue the search even in Gloomy Forest, where Fari-bur had already searched in vain. *Is it wrong to celebrate?* Boo wondered, for she couldn't stop herself smiling in front of Kuz'Aar and Bur-duun. They were not resentful; they would celebrate too, if their young lady returned, and Scuri'Boo had spent the hard winter searching for her alone. Uulor was also loud in his joy amid the rowdiness of the whole lea, excepting only the small group hidden in the long grass. Kuz'Aar and Bur-duun had slipped off with their band of rebels, for they had little to laugh at, indeed.

Kuz'Aar did the talking, as usual. 'Scuri'Boo is back. Floating Bliss and High Wind are still out there alone. It would be a disaster if Barzad were to return first.'

'Unless, of course, he returns with them,' Shubar interrupted.

'What do you think are the chances of that?' It sounded abrupt, but it was a genuine question. Shubar was silent.

'To return with them would be an admission of his mistake. He would be fallible.'

Shubar listened but was still hopeful. Bad as Barzad was, she couldn't believe a fairy could be so selfish, so vindictive. Yes, he was egotistical, but they all had failings. Kuz'Aar was lazy, Hazy Mellow was a lush, and Bor'Tem was a workaholic—so what?

'Well, we can do nothing until we know more,' said Bur-duun. 'Anyway, if we were to leave before Barzad returns, they might also return and find only him. We would never find them, and Barzad would have them all to himself to corrupt and destroy as he pleased. That would be the greatest disaster of all.'

Shubar interrupted again. 'That is very strong language, Bur-duun. I doubt Barzad means to destroy anyone.'

Grass Venture argued, 'But he will, whether he means to or not. Once he gets them all to himself, they'll be helpless. We can't leave.'

'They will never return. They are out there somewhere, and we should go to them. The longer we wait, the further away they will go.' No one spoke. It seemed the decision was made. Their meeting was adjourned, and they returned to the party separately, pretending they had always been there. But Hidden Thicket was not so easily deceived, and he was sorrowful.

His own family had been spared the pain Kuz'Aar and Bur-duun wilted under. How long would they last? How long would Tu'Hob and Tork cope? Tu'Hob slept only to dream of Scuri'Boo returning arm in arm with the two elopers. Hidden Thicket knew that; he stood over Tu'Hob as he slept. He stood over Kuz'Aar too; he knew of the plotting, the venom that dug into Kuz'Aar's soul and it made him afraid of what might come.

And far away, up in the high mountains, Resin Spell awoke late and still unrefreshed, despite the softness of spring. All was well, his parents were happy, but he was uneasy and they let him explain in time. He looked about, taking in the blue sky, Golden Orb, and the sweet smell of mountainous air. It was all he knew, but it was not perfect. Why did they live here alone? They should not live here alone.

'Tell me about the old place. Not before the long journey, the place before now.'

'Weedy Lea.'

'Why did you leave?'

'We've been through this. Barzad is a very difficult fairy. He would not let us be together, so we left.'

'Yes, but . . . now you are alone. Sometimes Mother has the blues.'

'That's just because I miss my friends and family. It'll pass.' Floating Bliss looked at High Wind with a weak smile. When she was lonely, she would go away to cry secretly but she had been found out.

'It won't pass,' Resin Spell said in his most authoritative voice. 'The old place sounds good in many ways. Maybe here is better, but it's not best. We need more fairies to dispel the loneliness.'

Resin Spell was right, of course. They imagined this place with many fairies, with no men to scare them and no Barzad to torment them. Resin Spell's grandparents could share in the joy of his being.

'Why should they be lonely for you down there and we be lonely for them up here? We should not be segregated. We should go to Weedy Lea and bring them back.'

'But what about Barzad? And they cannot make another journey; their wings are limp. Only you have strength in your wings.'

'Those are just obstacles. Your own wings are gaining strength, and what if we *do* have to walk? You did on your long journey.'

High Wind's head bent as he thought of De'Lyza and Vi'Shay. Walking all this way would take its toll on the other fairies, there was no doubt about that, but Resin Spell was right again. This was the place to be—or even a little further down the mountain, where the evergreens meet the bare-in-winter trees. Now he thought of Resin Spell, confident and engaging. Who better to lead them here? He would neither flinch at the thought of Barzad nor buckle under the weight of his own wisdom.

At night, Kuz'Aar and his rebels gathered to plot the final piece of their revenge. Bur-duun had already sent Barzad away; now all that remained was to be gone before he returned. A simple plan it seemed—simple but effective.

'Only one question makes us tarry. Do we await the elopers, or do we all go now and search them out? We must be sure of yesterday's decision.'

'I believe Kuz'Aar was right. They will not return if the despot, Barzad, is here alone. We must go and search for them.' This statement from Grass Venture made Dandelion Dew stare in horror. She had no idea there was so much against Barzad in his heart.

'Some will want to stay.' Bur-duun was thinking of poor Bor'Tem; she was such a sap for Barzad.

'Bor'Tem is on the council,' Kuz'Aar said, reading her mind. 'She will try to convince us all to stay. We must get the council on our side. We talk to Uulor first; he lacks confidence. We shake him till he shakes the others. Then, when everyone agrees, we all leave.'

Bur-duun was not convinced. Uulor would take a lot of shaking, especially if he knew the aim was revenge. Not a good enough reason to force elderly fairies into another long journey.

Dandelion Dew was afraid of what she was mixed up in, but she didn't dare voice her objection.

A cry in the dark startled them. Two cries.

'Curse o' the orbs, what is that?'

Another cry sounded.

'It's one of us, for sure.'

'Sounds like Uulor...'

Bor'Tem lay awake all night. She knew of the bad feeling in the lea. Soon they would be told to leave, and if Barzad ever returned, he would find an empty lea. She could wait forever, but he would never be hers. *So what?* she thought. *I deserve no less punishment for forcing Uulor into the lone life. And where is Uulor now? Not alone for sure. It is I who am alone.*

She would have tortured herself thus for hours more if the night were not broken by a sharp cry. Bor'Tem listened, heart battering her chest. Another cry quickly followed. 'Sounds like Uulor,' Bor'Tem said aloud, rising and running into the dark.

'Uulor!' A stab of responsibility came over her. 'Whatever's wrong, I probably did it to him.'

'Uulor! Where are you?'

Other fairies were waking. A tiny slit of light showed the horizon. Kuz'Aar came out from behind a clump of grass with Bur-duun in tow.

'Awake! Awake, everyone!'

'That *is* Uulor,' said Kuz'Aar.

Bor'Tem bumped him, confused in the dark. If only Barzad were here with his horn. She kept that thought to herself. Kuz'Aar would not much appreciate it.

'Uulor, we're here. Where are you?' Bur-duun found Bor'Tem groping blindly.

'Over here.' Uulor was nearby and no longer shouting. His voice was hoarse from the effort.

Bur-duun made for his direction and bumped him a second later. No, not Uulor.

'Who's that?' she asked, but she knew already.

Tu'Hob awoke from fitful sleep to shouting and boisterousness. He was not angered; he couldn't sleep anyway, and when he could, his mind was filled with nightmares of High Wind. Drowsily, he stumbled outside his den. All the fairies had gathered, and there was hustle and bustle and craning of necks. A voice alone spoke clearly but far away. Tu'Hob didn't recognise the voice. Eventually, when the noise died down, he could hear the last of what was said.

'We have welcome from the weeds and creatures, we have food aplenty, and so we have returned to bring you to the new land. My father is High Wind, my mother is Floating Bliss, and I am Resin Spell.'

# ANOTHER JOURNEY

Tired though they were, they set out almost immediately. It was morning, so why wait? They trusted the boy, and they would follow the lovers anywhere, so glad were they of their safe return. The luck of the fairies had changed. Tu'Hob was faint with relief that only a father could know, and Bur-duun also bloomed in her joy. Kuz'Aar not only had Floating Bliss back, but now all fairies would be leaving the lea forever; he had no need to persuade them. They followed, some not even seeing him who showed the way, just as they had followed Uulor many seasons ago. They spoke amongst themselves of Floating Bliss and High Wind's love, their romantic return, and the joyous birth of Resin Spell. Some skipped to the front of the procession, some rode seeds. Some got lost along the way and found the crowd again by asking feather-bills. None were afraid of the new place, of the uncertainty; they zigzagged along Windy Hill through the forest, higher and higher. Many creatures saw them and wondered at the sight, and surely if men had been there we would have noticed something strange about that wood as they travelled through it, leaving in their wake a line of colour and miracles ribboning through the trees. There was singing of songs and waving of arms and much affectionate hugging. Bor'Tem alone was unhappy, for she was leaving Thistle Town and Barzad forever. She was gracious and smiled so that none would know of her sorrow, but Bur-duun understood.

Resin Spell was no ordinary fairy; some marked this. Some commented on his confidence, but most talked of his wings, for they were strong. Indeed, he often flew a short distance ahead of them. Not everyone saw this, but everyone wanted to catch a glimpse, and they hoped that their own would gain strength enough to join him. And they were easily persuaded, when they grew tired, to move onwards. To find that steep hill far from men was their goal, and no tiredness would keep them from it. Even Vi'Shay and his old friend De'Lyza were loath to tarry but moved as though some energy propelled them. Resin Spell talked of this, for it was no secret that something gave him strength. His parents recalled aloud the recent feeling when they left Weedy Lea and found the new place together. They didn't follow their noses, they didn't even think about where they were going; they just followed the lead of some invisible thing.

And Uulor felt the pull. His worry came true, he had led them to the wrong place, but none of that mattered. Something else was guiding them. He was no longer expected to know everything. Perhaps now the council might agree the lone life was not his calling.

Thunderous rain began to fall, so they stopped. While they nourished themselves and rested, Kuz'Aar and Bur-duun sat grooming themselves, Uulor and Hidden Thicket whispered of the new life they might lead, and Bor'Tem and Stooping Reed talked of buttercup worship.

'We're heading upwards, to the top of the mountain, Stoop. Won't be no buttercups there.'

'Could we have been wasting our time all along? There can be no buttercup worship where there's no buttercups.'

'Perhaps Barzad was right,' suggested Bor'Tem. 'He always said we were wasting our time worshipping buttercups because they reminded us of Golden Orb. Should've just been worshipping Golden Orb.'

Genthem approached them softly, that he might ask Bor'Tem a question.

'If this young Resin Spell is leading us up the mountain, then the place Uulor chose was wrong. The old writings say a lone fairy leads us to our new life. Might he not be the lone fairy after all?'

Uulor and Hidden Thicket nearby, stopped whispering, and their eyes popped open in surprise. It was such a direct question. Most fairies held the council in reverence. It was common knowledge they had talked Uulor into his role, but to say the council were wrong seemed a little impolite. Everyone found their toes very interesting of a sudden. Bor'Tem had no answer. It was time for Uulor to come to her aid.

'My friends,' he began aloud so that the multitude listened. 'My friends, many of you are wondering why we are leaving again on another long journey. And some of you wonder why it is not I who lead. Well, the truth is, I don't know where we're going any more than you do. For a long time I've been afraid the lea was wrong, but it was too late before I realised. We had already settled. And for a long time the lone life felt wrong for me.' Here, Uulor paused and sought out Boo who sat with Scuri'Boo, and took the hand of Hidden Thicket, beside him.

'We on the council do our best, but we are not always right. Perhaps we set too much store by the fairy lore. Our ancient writings tell us a lone fairy will lead us to a world beyond limits—not this world of men but one of fairies. And here we are again, following the lead of one who knows, but he is not alone, for he is with his parents. We trust him, we warm to his charisma. We are hopeful when we see the strength of his wings—like a feather-bill. We look up to feather-bills as creatures of a greater gift, but in the feather-bill lore, fairies fly better! The fairy lore is not always right; neither are the council, and nor am I. We all often wonder who is the lonest of all fairies? Some of you think it is me; some of you think it is yourself.'

Here Uulor lowered his eyes so that they would not meet those of Kuz'Aar, who till recently thought it was himself,

Gor'Teeb, who till her romance with Ben'Tork thought it was herself, or Bor'Tem, who still did. 'But I tell you this, my friends. I've told you before, and I'll tell you again—it is not I.' Uulor sat down, and the rain stopped.

A silence followed. And a murmur followed the silence. Uulor rarely spoke unless it was important, so they took him seriously. He had led them to unrest and unhappiness, but if this new place could wipe that away, then great was Resin Spell and great was his high hill. The murmur filtered out to the edges of the group, losing its noise and leaving a ripple of contentment. Families began to sit in rings. Those with no family searched each other out and joined in solidarity, as though they were also families. They talked in their little groups of how Resin Spell spoke when first he came down the mountain. Those who heard everything described how his voice carried and his words gave joy and comfort. Those who heard less wished they had been nearer the front that they might have witnessed better, for it was history in the making. No one made any move to continue on; it was as though Resin Spell's words earlier and Uulor's words today were universally accepted as cause for celebration. And so they were.

Golden Orb began to set in shades of red and orange and grey, so they gathered themselves and started again to climb, that they might find some shelter for the night. There was excitement in the air, and a cool breeze dried their wings, allowing some to try a few flutters. None were as strong as Resin Spell, but most noticed a change, and that was enough for now. So they soldiered on, tired but glad. Evening became night, and with each day that followed they rose further up the mountain. There were some moments of unease. Once in the fading light of evening they noticed an old farmyard and were glad to leave it behind them in their travels. But the fairies need not have worried, because the men had long since left and all that remained were a few rusted machines and a rickety barn. Their journey was shared by feather-bills, bats, and other small creatures who were delighted to join the fairies, knowing that history was being made. Everyone understood the importance of what was happening. They were as one again. Rather than staying segregated by race, they remained together as a species. This made them stronger. Feather-bills chirped and chatted overhead, singing down to them of 'other fairy', whom they expected was Resin Spell, for he would often go ahead alone to be sure of their direction.

Bare-in-winter trees gave way to evergreen. The scent of pine needles filled the air. The song of feather-bills changed, and the blooms were different; sometimes the fairies moved inside the clouds, so high were they. Resin Spell walked more determinedly and his parents recognised the steps they had before taken. Food became scarcer, but they always had enough. And then at once, all in a moment together, Resin Spell, Floating Bliss, and High Wind sat. They were home.

The crowd gathered in a circle. *What should we do now?* they thought. *We should make places to live.* It was obvious, so they began the many days of discovery, finding little nooks and crannies to set up home, some in groups and some alone, but all together as a community. Older fairies began to feel the colour coming to their cheeks; there was no talk of revolt here. Everyone felt the magic of better health and happiness, and even Bor'Tem allowed herself a genuine smile now and then. Days became weeks, and weeks became months. Their wings gained strength enough to fly. The fairies settled and were glad, and Uulor no longer slept away from others, guarding them from some unknown misfortune. He joined their parties and was welcome, and all the while he spoke of the fairy lore in ways that showed a new interpretation.

'We are saved; we are blessed. Someone is watching over us, and it is not I.' But during one of his spiels, Ben'Tork shouted, "You've said yourself before that you *are* the lone. Remember your speech a long time ago, when you showed us Hidden

Thicket. You said, though you were the lonest of all fairies, you were also the happiest.'

And he who *was* lonest of all fairies laughed knowingly from his high vantage point, wings beating behind him as he clung carelessly to the treetops. He allowed an audible giggle of delight as he lay back against the bough, content and smiling. His eyes found Bor'Tem, whom he had come to love and a wave of joy filled his heart. Then he thought of the time when he had searched out the lovers, knowing they must have gone to Gloomy Forest, the one place of which he was afraid. He recalled the harrowing, dreary journey along the waterway, how there came from within his chest a howl that no fairy has uttered, and how it shook the banks in a way the bendy river will never forget. All the time he suffered, lonely and guilty, his strength was building, so he knew that, finally, he was doing right. He guided the lovers up the mountain, persuading feather-bills to eat what could be eaten, leaving no food behind so the fairies had to search higher and higher, and he orchestrated it unbeknownst to them. He made the flowers keep an eye on them while he flew back to the lea to needle Kuz'Aar in his sleep, whispering to him quietly, so Bur-duun would not wake. 'Go! Go and search for them.' And when the fairies would not listen to Kuz'Aar's persuasion, he had to do the same to Resin Spell. 'Go down! Go down the mountain and bring them here.' Once he was almost caught when High Wind stirred in his sleep.

His attention returned to the multitude below. They were still laughing at Ben'Tork's comment and the lone fairy agreed with them aloud, 'Yes, Uulor, you did say that, but you were wrong on both counts, for you are not the lonest of all fairies and it is I, Barzad, who am the happiest.'

Lightning Source UK Ltd.
Milton Keynes UK
UKOW031530260513

211243UK00010B/199/P